D1004731

MINISTRY OF DEATH

MINISTRY OF DEATH

JOHN BINGHAM

8257

WALKER AND COMPANY
New York

ISBN: 0-8027-5377-9

Library of Congress Catalog Card Number: 77-80631

Printed in the United States of America

10 9 8 7 6 5 4 3 2 1

CHAPTER 1

For some years Kenneth Vandoran had been known as Kenneth Ducane. They were years when he was almost continuously active in the field, and sometimes there was unwanted dramatic publicity, so the false name had been useful, not only for professional reasons, but to avoid awkward and tiresome questions at dinners and other social gatherings.

He had stuck to the name Ducane even when, on promotion, his outside activities had been largely curtailed. Reg Sugden had known him as Ducane during the nearly disastrous Moscow exploit, and he had been known as Ducane during the Cyprus business.*

But a year ago he had let his colleagues know that since he was now almost desk-bound, though not entirely, he had decided to become 'legitimate', as he put it. So Ducane had been relegated to the wings of the stage, and Vandoran had unobtrusively stepped forward to take his place. False passport and faked driving licence had been locked away in Vandoran's safe, and apart from occasional informal outbreaks Vandoran was legal again. Vandoran was his old self, and that meant he still suffered from periodic attacks of migraine.

It also meant that after one of these attacks he would be quite likely to have one of his usual rows with God.

Vandoran reckoned that if Dom Camillo could have rows with God, then so could he; admittedly the fictional Italian priest had a Special Relationship with the Creator,

* See *The Double Agent* and *Vulture in the Sun.*

but then again so had he. He conceded that on occasions it was a curious one, but he regarded it as firmly established by common usage.

So now he said, 'I know your Intelligence Organisation is, on the whole, better than mine, but I help against Your enemies now and again, don't I? Well, don't I?'

'Sometimes, in a minor way,' came the cautious answer.

'So why strike me down with piercing pains in the head, sickness, and half-vision? It's a waste of our time. You ever suffered from migraine?'

'Worse, actually.'

'Sorry.'

'*You* have pain-killing tablets.'

'I said I was sorry,' muttered Vandoran petulantly. 'And the tablets leave me muzzy. So now please clear my brain.'

The row with God was over but as a precaution, in case of a lack of prompt response due to lingering annoyance, Vandoran opened a desk drawer and took out a small bottle and swallowed a pill.

He sat still for a few minutes allowing time for the pill to work, for his mind to clear.

He was an ugly man, and knew it, and didn't mind. Some said he was in his mid-forties. Others added or subtracted a few years, and only Personnel Department and the National Health Insurance people knew the truth and they weren't telling.

Vandoran was of medium height, slightly built, brown-haired, with an undisciplined quiff of hair which stuck up not, as might have been expected, above his forehead but from behind, from the crown of his head, so that it looked like a dwarf feather worn by an Indian brave. His eyes were brown as almonds and the centres took up so much space that there was little or no room left for the white; even to talk of the whites of his eyes was a

6

courtesy, because they were as sallow as his skin, as though some of the colour of the eyes had leaked into the so-called whites. He had a small, ugly nose, a pointed chin and a wide mouth, thin-lipped and mobile, and so elastic that when he smiled his mouth stretched widely curving across his face. He was known as Froggie Vandoran to his staff, and knew he was, and thought it very appropriate, being totally devoid of vanity. He was usually dressed in some shade of brown, to match his eyes; his long, bandy legs, small body, and big out-turned feet added to the froglike appearance.

He was a frog with a good, cool brain, who could lie still for long periods, face hardly visible above the surface of the water, or in the grassy mud by the water's edge, and could tell the difference between an imitation butterfly on the end of a length of string and the real thing, and when in the end he sprang, long legs propelling the small body through the air, then the insect was a goner, and all that sometimes remained was a tattered end of a diaphanous wing, and a thin-lipped wide smile, and a slight movement or two of the jaws as he settled himself down again to wait and observe.

A predator like all frogs, he knew he was himself surrounded by predators, opposition Intelligence agents; and others too, men so obsessed with theories that they failed to see a third set of predators, less noisy, more cunning than themselves, using the democratic law to break down a society based on democratic law.

He rarely acted unless he was sure, and his staff knew that if he said, 'Spring!' then they could be fairly certain that their backs were guarded, and were comforted by the thought.

Froggie Vandoran never tossed a fellow frog to the foe – not if it could be avoided, that is; and if it couldn't be avoided then this was explained, which was doubtless

7

some consolation if not much. All Vandoran's frogs were trained to be reasonable amphibians and to expect the odd casualty.

They lived in a watery, dangerous world. It was their choice. They could always leave, perhaps on marriage, with a friendly shake of the flipper and a parting present of half a dozen flies, maybe a dozen if their record was good. Few did so.

After a minute or two he shook his head. There was no more pain and there was no more muzziness. But he sat staring across the room at the bookcase on the opposite wall, reviewing the current activities of his department and the overall situation, and was aware of a feeling of uneasiness and apprehension.

The cause was not that there were problems and threats and worries to be dealt with. The cause was exactly the opposite. The sky was blue, as far as the department was concerned, and there was not a cloud to be seen. This was not normal. To Vandoran, difficulties and challenges were part of the pattern for him. If there was a crowd of problems he was happy and unworried. To have no worries wasn't natural, and he became worried for lack of them.

If a heavenly tape-recorder had now been recording not his words but his thoughts, the resultant play-back would have been interesting to some, and irritating to others such as Reg Sugden, one of his best men, a practical Yorkshire type who would have declared that the best cure for Vandoran in his present mood was a dose of salts and a kick in the backside. The play-back would have thus recorded Vandoran:

'If everything is going perfectly, then the only change can be for the worse. I don't like it, no, I don't like it at all, no, I don't.'

The machine would not have recorded him thinking,

8

'I shall soon have to plot to kill a man', because he wasn't thinking it and there was no reason why he should have been. So in a way Vandoran was right and Sugden, he of the blunt words and thoughts, was wrong. It was all too quiet for safety.

And when the drama was over and the newspaper and television people produced their news stories and theories, the heavenly tape-recorder would duly record Vandoran as thinking, 'No, it wasn't like that, that wasn't at all the way things went.'

A similar piece of mechanism would have recorded exactly similar thoughts passing through the mind of Lawrence Brown, wherever he was, formerly Father Lawrence of the Church of Our Lady of Sorrows. Former residences, The Presbytery, Tarquin Road, East Clapham, and Flat 1a (basement), 312 Palace Road, East Clapham, which were half a mile away from each other in earthly distance, and half a world away in other matters.

CHAPTER 2

You could say that in the beginning there was a café, a
cup of weak coffee, and a humble toasted scone, for at
the time when Vandoran, for once late at the office, was
having his row with God, Father Lawrence Brown was
parking his old car on the yellow line outside a café
on the edge of Clapham called the New Speranza. Had
he been able to foresee the consequences he would almost
certainly have driven hastily on and found somewhere
else.

He knew that many such places incorporated the word
Speranza, meaning hope, and thought some were well
named in that you hoped for the best on the way in and
hoped that you would never have to revisit the place on
the way out. But this one looked clean and modern from
the outside and so it proved to be.

It was mid-morning and after the seven o'clock Mass
there had been little time to do more than change from
his vestments, and have a cup of tea in due course, before
leaving on the first of the visits to sick parishioners which
he had planned for that morning.

At about half-past eleven he felt hungry and a little
tired, and went in and sat at a table by the window.
From here he could keep an eye open for traffic wardens.
If one appeared he would leave some money on the
table and rush out, and hope that his priestly clothes
might cause the warden to turn a blind eye to the parking
offence and even allow him a few minutes to finish his
snack. He was aware that what seemed to be miracles

were not unknown, even in this day and age.

The waitress made no particular impression on him as she stood by his table taking his order. He was vaguely aware that she was perhaps in her early thirties, a few years younger than him, a girl of medium height with hazel eyes and a round, cheerful face with a good complexion, and shoulder length blonde hair.

It was only when she walked away from the table to fetch the coffee and scone that he felt any stirring of interest. He noted the way she held herself, erect, head up, chin slightly tilted. She looked neat and trim in her dark blue and white dress, and walked with a firm tread, and at each step, above the light-brown stockings, her thighs jerked rather than swayed, giving a hint of firm muscles beneath the short skirt. He watched her until she had reached the serving hatch, then hurriedly he went on scribbling into a notebook the results of his morning visits, occasionally glancing into the street in case a traffic warden had appeared.

His smoky blue eyes were thoughtful as he made a conscious effort to concentrate on his notes and not on carnal matters. Of such things he knew nothing except by hearsay. But he had a lively imagination; and it was his imagination that he now, and later for a time, tried to deflect from thoughts about the waitress, at first with some success. In the end, with no success at all.

During the busy daytime it wasn't too difficult. But at night it was a different matter. He soon recognised that his nightly prayers were becoming as dry as dust, and although he included a perfunctory appeal for help there was no heart in it, and he knew that directly he switched out the bedside lamp his resistance to his imaginings in regard to Mavis Bailey, as she said she was called, was a formality. Soon he dispensed even with the formality.

Several times a week now he felt the need for mid-

11

morning sustenance at the Speranza café. Indeed, during this period sick parishioners within easy distance of the Speranza café were full of praise for him, pointing out how diligent he was in visiting them. They had never had it so good. Neither, in a way, had Father Lawrence.

When he dropped in at the Speranza, Mavis Bailey now greeted him cheerfully as 'Father Lawrence, hinny'. Hinny, he gathered, was a Newcastle Geordie word, a warm, friendly word, slightly similar to 'mate' in the south. It was after a month of periodic coffees and scones that she staggered him by speaking to him in a most remarkable manner.

She had asked him where he had parked his car, and he had said, 'Outside, as usual.'

'On the yellow line? You'll get a parking ticket, hinny!'

'Maybe yes, maybe no. Got to live dangerously sometimes,' he answered.

'Whey ye boogger!' she said.

It was said in an admiring way. He blinked.

'I beg your pardon?'

He wasn't shocked, but astonished. She saw his surprise and laughed.

'It doesn't mean the same up Newcastle way, Father Lawrence, hinny. Depends how you say it, see? Tone of voice, see? Instead of "good old you", we say, "*Whey*, ye boogger!" But if we tick a bloke off for trying it on we smack his face and say "Whey, ye *boogger!*"'

She smiled again, hazel eyes dancing.

'You can make a whole sentence out of it, you know.'

'You can?'

She nodded. 'There's this bloke who tells his pals that the boss is a cunning old fox, who's done his rivals in the eye again. He says, "Whey, ye booggers, the old boogger's booggered the booggers again, the boogger." Complimentary, see?'

After that, when he called in for his coffee and scone she would say, 'Morning, Father Lawrence, hinny,' and he would politely reply, 'Whey, ye boogger,' and they'd both smile, because there is nothing more binding than a common knowledge of 'in' talk.

Then suddenly, without a word of warning, she came no more.

A strange waitress, pleasant but angular, took his orders and walked with a ragged, gawky gait to the serving hatch.

Nobody knew why Mavis Bailey had gone.

She had given no reason. Waitresses came and went. Nobody was interested except Father Lawrence, and he kept his interest to himself. He heard no more of her for three months.

She had told him she lived in his parish. It seemed she was a lapsed Catholic, but each Sunday he took extra care to make his sermon a thing of beauty, and as he delivered it he scanned the sea of faces before him on the off-chance, looking for blonde hair and a pair of hazel eyes, hoping that she might have attended Mass if only to say to him as she went out of church, 'Hello, Father Lawrence, hinny!'

He knew what he would have replied, and he had rehearsed the tone of voice to use. He would have whispered, 'Whey, ye boogger,' in a tone to indicate a mixture of surprise and genuine pleasure. But though he had rehearsed the tone, he had no chance to use it. They filed passed him at the church door after Mass, greeting him and going their separate ways.

Now that he did not see her, he fell asleep more easily at night, until the evening of 1 April.

According to the roster he was due to hear confessions from 4 p.m. to 6 p.m. on that All Fools' day. He never liked hearing confessions, especially not from people who thought they were dying but later recovered. They often posed serious conflict between the duty of a citizen and the duty of a priest. But he knew that the seal of the confessional had to remain inviolate, worrying though it could be. He hated doing even a normal, undramatic stint in the stuffy confessional box – at least after the first six months, by which time the novelty had worn off and he no longer felt himself to be, in a way, exercising some kind of delegated godly authority. Although there were guidelines he felt desperately lonely, a fragment painfully striving to help other fragments to attain inner peace and spiritual tranquillity, deeply conscious of his lack of worldly experience and aware of the time limit. They sat patiently waiting their turns on the bench outside the box. How long had he to cope with each problem? Three minutes, perhaps four, to listen, consider the problem and give advice, penance, admonition, encouragement.

Almost worse than the strain of trying to cope with a difficult problem in a limited time was the boredom of listening to what seemed total normality, the recital, endlessly repeated over the weeks, months, and years, of a mixture, with some startling exceptions, of trivialities and crude excesses; of listening to voices he often recognised outlining sins he knew would be repeated, even as he gave an absolution which in effect was useless because, apart from making amends, it depended upon a firm resolve to reform, which obviously wasn't there. It couldn't be there, or he wouldn't hear the same voices repeating the same things, year after year, or month after month, or week after week. You didn't need to know their names, though almost inevitably, in certain cases, you did know who they were, because voices can be as distinctive as names, and you met them outside at bazaars or socially. So back they came with their tales of petty thieving, drunkenness, missed masses, lies, adultery and fornication.

Once, in his early inexperienced days, he had touched upon the question of repetitions and an obvious lack of firm resolve not to sin again, and had got himself into a tight corner with a man whose voice was unfamiliar.

'I will give you absolution,' he had said. 'But you must ask yourself if you have often committed this sin before, and if therefore your promise not to sin again is worth saying. If not ....' He did not finish the sentence. He knew he did not need to. There was silence for a few seconds. Then a cultured voice said,

'You are implying that you believe the absolution you will give me now may be invalid?'

'It is for you to ask yourself that question, and for you to answer it.'

'You imply that the needed firm resolution is not there. Therefore I should not come to confession, that it is a waste of your time and mine, that I should stay away, that God has not forgiven me?'

Father Lawrence stirred uneasily and felt the blood rushing to his face, and in desperation he said a sudden silent prayer of his own, quickly, not bothering to frame it properly, saying the first words that flashed through his mind, sending the call for help hurtling on its way, 'Lord, I've made a pig's ear of this one. Lord, I've mucked it, tell me what to say.'

Almost at once he had heard himself answering, 'Even if you cannot make a perfect act of contrition, even if, when you say "I am sorry I have sinned and I promise never to sin again", you have in your heart some doubt about the last six words, you should still come to confession, for it may be that by making the effort to come, and in this holy building, you will one day indeed make

15

a perfect act of contrition, and all will be well. Go in peace.'

He had given absolution because there was no time for a debate, and heard the man scramble out of the cubicle. He had never come back. Perhaps he had gone in future to some less pernickety priest.

But on this All Fools' day things were very different. He settled himself in the confessional with the tired feeling of one who knows he is likely to have a hard slog ahead, and in due course glanced briefly sideways out of the corner of his eye. He could dimly make out, through the close wire mesh which separated priest from penitent, the head of a child; and a childish voice smelling of peppermint said earnestly, 'Bless me, Father, for I have sinned,' and he made the usual response.

She had, it seemed, been rude to her mother, and cheated at exams by looking at the paper of a child seated next to her. She had also stolen three pence out of the money her father had given her for a church collection and spent it on chocolate.

Father Lawrence sighed and cleared his throat and said, 'Do you love your mother?'

Yes, she did, of course she did, she couldn't say anything else.

'Do you love Jesus?'

Yes, she did. What else could she say?

'Jesus loved his mother. He was never rude to her. He was never rude to anybody, though He sometimes reprimanded people; not even in His agony, not even to the robber on the cross beside Him; and Jesus never stole. But in cheating at exams you steal the work of a classmate, and when you take money given to you for the collection at church you take money which was for Jesus's work, see? Now make a perfect act of contrition, and for your penance say two Our Fathers, and three Hail Marys.

Take your chewing gum if you have parked any in the confessional.'

A few seconds later she was away. Scuttle, scuttle.

A pause. The movement of a cumbersome body. Heavy breathing. And suddenly he felt queasy and it was all he could do to stop himself from retching as a smell of stale beer, with a trace of garlic, filled the confessional.

It was all right for the penitents, he thought, they came and said their little piece, and they went. But the priest was stuck there. However bad the smells he couldn't cut and run.

All the smells weren't nauseating. Some of them were unpleasant but tolerable, like old, wet clothing, or stale cigars, or the mustiness of very elderly people, or scent, and not all the scents were cheap and sickly; some were heavy, some very pleasant, but not many. The beery man's sins were not unusual, a mixture of extra-matrimonial sex and dishonesty to pay for it. Father Lawrence Brown's exhortations ran along old familiar grooves.

Then suddenly he knew that Mavis was in the box by his left shoulder. He could smell her scent and recognise her north-country voice. After the preliminaries he heard her murmur softly,

'I have had carnal thoughts about a man to whom I am not married, and whom I can't marry.'

'Are you married? Divorced?'

'No.'

'Is he married? Divorced?'

'Neither.'

'Are you in love with him?'

'I think so.'

'Have you any reason to think that he has similar feelings about you?'

There was a pause. The confessional still held the

smell of her scent. She was breathing quickly, and he heard her move.

'He has done nothing, said nothing. How should I guess his feelings?'

'It is a dangerous situation unless you hope to marry him in the Church, and even then you must be careful lest your immortal soul—'

She did not let him finish.

'I do not hope to marry him, because he cannot marry me.'

'Is he healthy – physically and mentally?'

'Yes – very.'

'He is unmarried, you say, and you are free...?'

He let the implications hang in the air. After a while, when she said nothing, he sighed and said,

'It is a matter for you and him. Meanwhile—'

'It is not a matter for me and him,' she said tartly. 'It is a matter for the Catholic Church.'

Father Lawrence stiffened automatically, alert, ready to be defensive. But at first he said nothing. The reaction was partly instinctive because he had not yet completed his spiritual break, and partly because a stab of jealousy surged over him and he needed time to think. To gain time he said,

'Tell me why.'

'There is good reason.'

'Tell me.'

'Because he is a Roman Catholic priest,' she replied tensely. 'That's why he can never marry me – even if he wanted to.'

'A priest, ordained, and in the service of God—' he began mechanically, once more to gain time, but she cut him short.

'What God?' she asked acidly.

He heard her shuffle, alter her position, but what he

18

mostly heard was the thudding of the blood in his ears as his pulses quickened with excitement. He said hurriedly but softly,

'We cannot discuss our problems here, Mavis, hinny.'

'Where then?'

He hesitated, thinking of the roster, thinking of the pattern of life at the presbytery.

He sensed how the seconds were slipping by in silence, that she was waiting eagerly for an answer of the kind she hoped for. And he knew it was a point of no return, that although in some measure he had managed to sublimate his feelings during her absence it had been a dreary period for him, a dry desert patch in his life, and that if they did not meet again soon she was likely to abandon him for good.

'Where then?' she repeated, a little impatiently.

'Tomorrow afternoon at the presbytery.'

He was aware that it had only been a token struggle. He was also aware that nobody else would be in the house, not even the elderly housekeeper who cooked and cleaned.

'Four-thirty, if you can make it. Coffee and toasted scones, and I will wait on *you* for a change.'

'O.K.'

He heard her sigh, and imagined it was a sigh of relief or pleasure. Then there was the sound of movement, then silence, and she was gone, and only the smell of her scent lingered for a while. He had once commented on it in the Speranza café, and she had said the scent was called 'Piège'. He had looked the word up in a French dictionary.

He found it meant 'Trap'.

He walked into this particular trap with his eyes wide open, ready and eager to spring the catch himself. From the moment he made the appointment he was never in any doubt about the outcome.

For a long time now he had been carrying out his duties meticulously but only mechanically, knowing in his heart that the end would come soon, not knowing how, not knowing exactly when, only knowing that the fuse was prepared and awaiting the spark.

Now he knew how, and when, and that the spark would fire the fuse at 4.30 p.m. that day.

She rang the bell punctually and stood on the door-step, demurely dressed in a navy-blue skirt and coat and a white blouse as befitted a caller at such an hour and at such a place, and she wore a cross on a thin gold chain round her neck, and her blonde hair fell about her shoulders contrasting with the blue coat. She even managed a shy, hesitant smile when he opened the door, and as she followed him in and watched him close the door and lead the way to the sitting-room.

'There is nobody else here,' he said quietly, and turned and stood in front of her and watched her raise her eyes and put her arms round his neck. He kissed her full on the lips a long time, and held her close, and it was the first time he had kissed a woman apart from his mother and sister, and he felt what seemed like electricity flowing through his body, and held his breath, and even felt a little dizzy, and did not want to release her.

When he did so he said,

'Are you quite sure?'

'Quite sure.'

'How?'

'I just know. It's not a question of me. Are *you* quite sure? – I've a baby, remember.'

'So sure that I applied for a passport – months ago – so that we could go to Portugal for our, you know, honey-moon. I wasn't sure of *you*, of course. It was just – a hopeful precaution, part of a dream that might come true. Why did you go away? Thinking it over?'

'Thinking it over,' she lied and nodded happily, glad that he had provided her with a ready-made excuse.

She couldn't tell him about the baby, not at that moment, and had mentally fabricated some tale about her mother being ill. The excuse he had provided for her sounded dignified and plausible and she snapped it up eagerly.

She kissed him again.

'When?' she asked at length.

'Three weeks' time. Yesterday I booked the car on the car-ferry.'

She looked at him admiringly, hazel eyes shining.

'Sure of yourself, weren't you?'

'I didn't need to be psychic, did I? Not after what you said in church.'

Later, much later, Sugden said to Vandoran,

'I heard he never tried to seduce her, though she went there once or twice more, fixing up details and all that. I believe it. He wouldn't have known how to begin. And *she* never tried to seduce *him*.'

'Too clever,' Vandoran said shortly. 'Given the circumstances, that lad never had a chance.'

The evening after his decision, Father Lawrence carefully made out a list of names and addresses and said to his curate, Father Davidson,

'I have been feeling somewhat jaded, and I have accepted an invitation to visit Portugal in about two weeks' time.'

Father Davidson looked up from a sermon he was preparing. He seemed mildly disconcerted. Guessing the reason Father Lawrence Brown said, 'I will try and get hold of somebody to help you out. If I can't, I'm afraid you will have to cope as best you can.'

'How long will you be away?'

'I can't tell you exactly. Some little time.'

'Couple of weeks?'

'Perhaps longer. I'm sorry, but I need a change. I *do* need a change,' he repeated slowly. He handed his curate the list of names and addresses.

'These are some people who would appreciate a call, if you have time. Some are sick. By the way, there's a nice clean little café, the New Speranza, I've found in East Clapham. I recommend it.'

Father Davidson hesitated, then took the list, saying,

'You sound as though you were handing over your last will and testament, Father Lawrence.'

Father Lawrence Brown laughed and said lightly, 'It's just that I like to prepare for all possibilities. Anybody can be run over by a bus, and anyway, as I say, I am not exactly sure when I shall be back. One does not like to leave loose ends.'

Father Davidson went on with the notes for his sermon. Privately, he thought Father Brown was being a little inconsiderate, what with some First Communions in the offing, not to mention Easter. Yes, what about Easter and the heavy duties involved? He spoke his thoughts, a trifle indignantly.

'What about Easter, Father?'

'I have told you I will try to get some help for you, Father.'

Father Davidson looked up. Father Lawrence Brown had flushed pink. He's a good and hard-working priest, Father Davidson thought, but quick tempered, everybody knows that. So he said no more about Easter and went on preparing his sermon.

When he had finished he ventured one last question, 'Who's the friend, Father? Do I know him?'

'Somebody I've known casually for some time. Off and on. The name would mean nothing to you.'

Father Brown had flushed again, and was tight-lipped. Father Davidson was surprised. He considered his question had been an innocent enough one.

'Well, I hope you have a good time, Father,' he said and got up to go into the kitchen to fry their fish because it was the housekeeper's day off.

'Oh, I shall,' said Father Brown. 'Thank you, I *shall*.'

He carried out his duties punctiliously till the day of his departure. On the Saturday before he left he heard confessions for the last time. There were the usual dreary recitals, relieved only by one interruption.

He knew it was her without catching a glimpse of her blonde hair through the mesh. He could smell the scent she was wearing, called 'Piège', and he was filled with a moment of panic, wondering if she had changed her mind. For a moment he stopped breathing, then he heard her voice,

'Is it all right for tomorrow?'

'It is,' he replied softly, and breathed again, and heard his heart thudding with excitement.

'About eleven-thirty in the morning, after Mass?'

'Agreed.'

'By the side of the new Redgate Underground station?'

'I will park the car and my suitcases nearby, and then walk to Mass here. Agreed? I will meet you at the station entrance. Stay in the confessional a little longer now, darling. Otherwise people will think you just popped in to say good evening.'

'Do you love me, darling?' she whispered.

'Deeply.'

'More than you love God?'

He repeated her words in the confessional when he

first listened to her there, and took the last and final leap, and felt no qualms.

'What God?' whispered Father Lawrence Brown, still Roman Catholic priest of the Church of Our Lady of Sorrows.

There had to be no God, otherwise the long-term prospects were too terrifying to contemplate. He heard her snigger. Then she was gone, leaving only the smell of her scent, the name of which in English was 'Trap'.

The bait had been irresistible.

It was over now, his last Mass finished, and he turned to face the congregation. Tall, dark-haired and handsome, with a small neat beard, the vestments of a priest enhanced his appearance, and he knew it.

In the early period of his priesthood, when making his own confessions, he had several times confessed to the sin of vanity, received absolution, and in those days had prayed that he might be granted the strength to expunge vanity from his character.

But it hadn't worked.

He had remained conscious of his slim, elegant figure, his dark, wavy hair, cleft chin, and the blue eyes whose cool, thoughtful gaze was no mirror to his passionate soul.

So now, at the end, when he faced the congregation for the last time, he was aware not only of the drama of the moment but also of his own splendid appearance, and thought it fitting that a beam of sunshine from the windows above the choir should envelop him, emphasising the healthy glow of his skin and the green of his vestments.

The fear of attack, mutilation, death even, had not yet touched him. There would be a row with the hierarchy, of course, but that would blow over.

He was enjoying it all, and lingered for a few seconds. In the modern style he should tell them in English that they should go, Mass was over. In the old days when he was a younger priest the Latin words were, *'Ite Missa est.'* Suddenly it seemed fitting to him that he should end his priesthood in Latin, as he had begun it, and he was tempted to do so.

In the sea of faces he caught sight of the fawn-like features of an M.P., Edward Mallow, and the heavy, square tortoiseshell-type spectacles of a local councillor, Councillor Davis. He didn't know if Mavis Bailey was there. He hadn't spotted her when he gazed around during the sermon, but he felt sure she would be present, somewhere, admiring his last great performance. And it had indeed been a great performance, not an inflection over-stressed, not a gesture out of place.

Professional but graceful, that's what it had been.

But now it had to end. The church was deathly quiet, except for a moment when a baby whimpered and was hushed by its mother. A very faint, lingering smell of incense pleased his nostrils. He had been standing there motionless for ten seconds, and ten seconds was quite a long time. Women would be thinking, well, go on, get on with it, I've got to get the meat in the oven, and men would be thinking, get a move on, the pubs will soon be open.

It was time to ring the curtain down on the last performance, and he was certain that he would say, *'Ite Missa est.'* What is more, yielding totally to the theatrical drama of the situation, he went off-ritual, and raised his arms to shoulder level, palms extended to his audience, Christ-like, and stood motionless for a few seconds as he prepared to say the words, glad that the sunshine still spotlighted him.

But he did not say the words then.

A man at the end of a pew at the back of the church shouted loudly and angrily, 'To hell with the Pope!' and got to his feet.

Father Lawrence froze, arms still extended.

He had noticed the man during the sermon, and idly thought he was a newcomer, perhaps a new resident, a new regular member of the congregation. Or perhaps just a holiday-maker. He was a middle-aged, short, bald, red-faced stocky man in a brown suit and, although it was a warm spring day, he wore a brown herringbone-patterned overcoat.

The man began to run up the aisle towards the altar. When he was a few feet from Father Lawrence he stopped and took something out of his pocket and threw it.

The egg struck Father Lawrence Brown on the right shoulder, cracked and fell messily to the ground, then a rotten tomato hit Father Lawrence on the forehead, and squashed itself, and the juice ran down his face. The man shouted once more, 'To hell with the Pope!' and added, 'Down with the Scarlet Woman of Rome!' and turned and ran.

The woman with the baby screamed. Two men tried to stop the man at the door but he brushed them aside. Now there was a murmuring and a stirring of feet as bewildered faces turned to watch the man escape.

Father Lawrence's first instinct was to wipe away the tomato juice. But he didn't. He remained stock still as the juice gleamed on his face. Then, when the hubbub had died down a little and all eyes were again on him, he said quietly but firmly, *'Ite Missa est.'*

In retrospect, he knew that the incident had not spoiled his last performance. As he had stood there, arms extended, bearded, Christ-like, and later calmly concluded Mass, he knew that his second instinctive reactions had made it his finest hour.

CHAPTER 3

The defection of Father Lawrence Brown from the Roman Catholic Church for the love of Mavis Bailey affected different people in different ways.

To the national Press he was not so much God's defector as God's gift to news editors, because he was tall and dark and handsome, blue eyed, with clean-cut features, type cast for the role of a priest who had 'sacrificed all for love'.

To earthly-minded men in public houses, in sea ports, on building sites and other such places, men who had seen published snapshots of Mavis Bailey, he was just a bloke who carried his conscience in an unconventional place. They didn't even read much beyond the headlines before turning to the sports pages.

The Church's reaction was naturally one of regret but not undue surprise, because this sort of thing happened now and again, and probably always would. Some Roman Catholic priests, and some Anglican clergymen, seemed accident-prone. Sometimes it was sex, sometimes drink, and sometimes both, and that's all there was to it; and there was nothing one could do about it except utter sorrowful but soothing noises to the faithful, with here and there a reminder that man was frail and beset by the temptations of Satan.

But when certain other people learned that ex-Father Lawrence not only did not believe in Satan but did not believe in God either, and was now an agnostic and probably at heart an atheist, various implications suddenly loomed on the horizon, each like a small cloud no bigger than the United States of America. Even then it took a day or two until the deadly penny dropped.

The first to be struck was Mr Edward ('Good old Eddie') Mallow, left-wing Conservative Member of Parliament for East Clapham, London. He was just about to hole an easy two-feet putt when the penny dropped with a sound like a poor man's atom bomb. So he missed the putt, to his partner's annoyance, who had £5 on the game.

Councillor John Davis was in the middle of a witty speech after a Rotarian lunch when he suddenly faltered and, to the alarm and dismay of his audience, felt for his brandy glass, which was not unusual, but his hand was shaking, and Councillor Davis was an experienced and far from nervous speaker. He recovered, but there was no more fun in his speech which, in fact, petered out – and that would be putting it mildly.

Ron Flint, being not as fast on the uptake as the others, was mentally undisturbed until after closing hours at the Sportsman's Bowl on the same day, where he was playing pontoon and drinking with four friends in a back room at the pub, with the permission of the landlord whose permission, in turn, was winked at by the police because it saved a good deal of time to know various places where people could often be picked up, some of whom would broadly be termed gangsters and others just normal crooks and even dull burglars.

Ron Flint had just laid two cards face up on the table, an ace and a king, which would normally have produced a smile on his thick-lipped rubbery face and a snarl of triumph from his throat. Instead, as the delayed thought occurred to him he muttered, 'Jeeze!' an American exclamation which he had picked up from films, and the blood momentarily left his face.

28

'What's up then?' asked Len Wilson, a thin man with a long nose, a cadaverous face and thinning, greasy dark hair.

'Nowt, nowt much,' Ron Flint replied, and rubbed his stomach. 'Touch o' belly wauch.' He was of north-country origin, but usually spoke with what some might have called Cockney patois, though it wasn't really. In moments of stress, as now, he was inclined to revert to northern expressions.

'Perhaps it's them mussels you ate,' said Len Wilson.

'Aye, and 'appen it ain't,' muttered Ron Flint, and got to his feet. 'Who's for a nip of Scotch?'

They all accepted. Len Wilson stroked the bald patch on the top of his head where the oily, black hair failed to meet. He knew Ron Flint lived by the old Yorkshire adage, 'Hear all, say nowt; sup all, pay nowt; and if tha does owt for nowt, do it for tha sen.' So Len Wilson knew Ron Flint was seriously upset, seeing that he was buying a round of whiskies.

Fear, violence and death can stalk their victims in strange disguises, creeping up through the undergrowth, unnoticed by on-lookers because, until they are on the move, spectators do not even know they are about. Indeed the stealthy approach can be further obscured by amusing aspects: a Member of Parliament missing a putt amid chaffing and laughter; a stout town councillor muffing his speech, maybe because he has drunk too much; a crook with sudden stomach-ache just as good fortune attends him at cards.

Mr Edward Mallow, M.P., Councillor Davis and Ron Flint had each smelt danger. Father Lawrence Brown, in good health, would never have dreamed that evil things were to make him a very bad insurance risk; one which no sensible company would accept; which, since the

Inquisition is no longer active to kill defectors, might have seemed unlikely.

Having a much better brain than most of his former flock Lawrence Brown did not need a subsequent sentence in a newspaper to make him realise that he could now be in acute physical danger. At first it was a casual thought, then it recurred, and what were at first niggling worries began permanently to tease his mind, and they were nothing to do with the religion which he had cast off, involved no tormented Christian soul-searching about the spiritual correctness or otherwise of what he had done. He told himself at first that they were connected with his social and ethical conscience and whether he should go to the police but he didn't entirely convince himself; and because he had a better brain he saw his peril long before the backroom boys at the pub, and the others, had realised their own.

Most of the time he persuaded himself that it was all his imagination, that such things couldn't happen, at any rate not in Britain – or even Portugal. But now and again, if he woke in the early hours of the morning on his so-called honeymoon, he saw no reason why they shouldn't. Occasionally in his heart of hearts he knew that they could because various things can make various people afraid and therefore desperate and dangerous. Once, in a very black moment, he was sure they did happen and would again, and he sweated; and because old, almost sub-conscious habits die hard, and he was half asleep, he found himself automatically saying the last line of the 'Hail Mary': 'Holy Mary, Mother of God, pray for us sinners now and in the hour of our death, amen.' He kept sleepily repeating the words, 'and in the hour of our death, amen, and in the hour of our death, amen, and in the hour of our death, amen', until eventually he fell asleep, and awoke next morning ashamed of his superstitious lapse. He said nothing to Mavis to worry her and spoil their holiday.

Had he spoken of this to anybody he would have said that Mavis and her child needed him above all else and it was thus his duty to remain alive. Half of his mind believed it. The other half conceded the truth: he was scared stiff.

He knew the reason, being aware that at least three people would not only welcome his death but might well be willing to lend a friendly neighbourhood hand to anybody inclined to bring it about.

He first came face to face with his fear, recognising it for what it was, on the evening of the second day of the holiday. It had been a perfect day. Swimming under a cloudless sky, the water still cold but the sun warm as they lay on the beach. Then a short drive in the old Anglia to some nearby pine woods for a picnic. Bringing the Anglia over on the S.S. *Eagle* had been expensive but worth it. Then they had snoozed in the sun, then driven to a former monastery near Sesimbra and gone over it. It aroused no religious qualms. There were none left in him, only other qualms aroused by the knowledge of the information in his head and what, if anything, he should do about it. More particularly, what other people might do about it.

They were changing for dinner when the bedside telephone buzzer sounded, and he lifted the receiver and heard the receptionist say,

'There is a gentleman wishes to see you, sir.'

His heart jumped. He swallowed and said,

'Who? What's his name?'

There was a short pause, then the receptionist said,

'He says you do not know him, his name would mean nothing to you he says, sir. He says it is important to meet you. He will wait for you at a table at the far end of the garden. He is wearing a light-blue suit.'

'Thank you,' said Lawrence Brown non-committally, and replaced the receiver. Mavis was seated in front of the mirror doing her hair.

'Shall I go down and see him?' he asked.

'Why not? He'll only seek you out if you don't. Order me a Campari, love. Perhaps it's an emissary from the Pope offering to make you a bishop if you'll return. Come back, Larry, all is forgiven,' she said facetiously, and giggled.

'Envoy of the Pope wearing a light-blue suit – as disguise,' muttered Lawrence Brown, and wandered to the window overlooking the garden. He saw the man sitting at a little table. He was small, seemed squarely built and swarthy, and was smoking a cigarette. Parked in a narrow road beyond the garden was a red sports car. He wondered if the car belonged to the man. He also wondered if all his life now, in view of what he knew and others knew he knew, he would always be apprehensive about meeting strangers alone in secluded parts of gardens, or anywhere else where he could be.... He hesitated, believed the expression was 'knocked off', and said the words softly.

'What did you say?' asked Mavis.

'Nothing. I'll go and see what he wants,' he said reluctantly, and made his way thoughtfully downstairs and out into the garden. As he approached, the man rose and extended a hand. When he spoke and announced his name Lawrence Brown judged him to be half English, half Portuguese.

'Father Brown?'

'Mr Brown now. Lawrence Brown.'

'James Jarvis, Lisbon correspondent of the English *Sunday News*, sir, at your service, sir.'

Jarvis sat down.

Lawrence Brown remained standing.

'I don't think I want any service, thank you. How did you know I was here?' It had to happen some time but he was interested in clearing up the details. He was also relieved. It was tiresome but could have been so much worse.

James Jarvis seemed surprised at the question.

'Passenger lists, sir, port authorities, sir, we got contacts, sir, we keep our eyes open, so does our London office, sir. Easy, really. Our London office instructs me—'

'Nothing to say, Mr Jarvis. Sorry.'

He began to turn away, but stopped abruptly because James Jarvis had said, 'Not for five thousand pounds, Father?'

'What for, Mr Jarvis?'

'Your story, Father. Three instalments for the paper, that's all – and we'll write it for you. You just give us a few facts, we'll write it. Not now, of course, don't want to spoil your holiday, sir. Directly you get back to London get in touch with our features editor. He'll fix it. Think about it?'

'I'll think about it,' he said slowly. He would, too. Having left the Church his income was now £00.00 per annum.

'I'm instructed to give you this, sir – one hundred pounds,' and he extended a bundle of notes.

'What for?'

'For nothing, Father, that's the beauty of it – for nothing, for agreeing to do nothing till you get back. By nothing we mean nothing, like talking to other papers, see?'

Lawrence Brown shook his head gently. 'I don't need that, Mr Jarvis. You have my word I'll do nothing. I'm on holiday.'

33

James Jarvis looked at him suspiciously with his dark, almost black, eyes. He said, 'Well, remember, sir, we'll offer more than anybody else.'

Lawrence Brown believed him The *Sunday News* was a popular and very successful and enterprising newspaper.

It was a lovely holiday. Two weeks of it, and the weather was wonderful, Mavis was wonderful, and he enjoyed a good slug of Portuguese wine in the evenings. He wasn't afraid all the time. Far, far from it. He had plenty of things to occupy his mind, other than something which, all in all, was very unlikely to happen.

She was a sweet girl – usually bright and cheerful and always affectionate and loving and he still found her Newcastle Geordie accent attractive. She was friendly to everybody, sometimes a little too friendly, he thought, but life to her was for living, and poetry and classical music and art was stuff for high-brows.

He had once said affectionately that she was a real little extrovert but she had not commented, looking at him in a bemused way, not knowing what he meant, wondering what the word meant, wondering if it was an insult, not liking to ask; and on another occasion, when picnicking beside a little river at the foot of a hill, he had stretched out happily, and murmured, ' "Here with a Loaf of Bread beneath the Bough, A Flask of Wine, a Book of Verse – and Thou Beside me singing in the Wilderness – And Wilderness is Paradise enow." ' He was almost ashamed to be so corny, and it wasn't until he heard her reaction that he fully appreciated the totality of her poetic ignorance.

'Well, I'm not going to sing,' she murmured sleepily. 'What's all that about?'

'You know – from the *Rubáiyát*.'

'The ruby what?'

'A collection of verses, darling, by Omar Khayyám.'

'Who's she, Old Ma thing? Who's Old Ma What'sit?' she asked half-asleep.

He laughed delightedly and patted her thigh, wondering whether she was teasing him, sometimes, as perhaps now, deliberately cultivating her non-culture.

'A Persian poet, sweetheart – he lived nearly a thousand years ago.'

'Foreigner,' she muttered. 'Don't know him. Before my time.' She giggled, and fell asleep.

He looked down on her body dappled by the sunshine piercing through the trees, lissom and supple, and knew he only had to fondle her and she would raise her head and her lips meet his own, but you didn't do these things in Portugal, he believed, certainly not in Spain, not in the open air, not in daylight, not unless you wanted to find yourself in trouble with the authorities.

Upstream, about fifty yards away, a powerful-looking brown car had stopped on a little grey bridge, and a woman and two men were leaning over the parapet looking downstream either at him and Mavis or at the view. Probably at both, he thought irritably, and why shouldn't they? On the other hand, why should they? The view from the bridge was not all that unusual. He watched them move to the side of the bridge, stoop down, and pick up what might be some giant fir-cones three times as big as English ones. They went back to the car and it drove off, and he felt at peace again and slipped down beside Mavis, thinking of another of Old Ma What'sit's verses: 'Ah, fill the Cup: – what boots it to repeat How Time is slipping underneath our Feet: Unborn To-MORROW, and dead YESTERDAY, Why fret about them if To-DAY be sweet!'

It was sweet all right and, as to tomorrow, he looked forward to evenings by the fireside when he would be able to lure her educational innocence into rich avenues which she could later explore herself; and so she would, because she was bright enough. Later in the evening they would go to bed and she would lure his own comparative innocence into other rich avenues, not cultural within the meaning of the definition, but valuable in their way, complementary to his own different knowledge and abilities.

He didn't speak the lines aloud because he knew that in her present intellectual state she wouldn't understand them and might ask exactly what time of day it really was, whether it was or whether it wasn't slipping underneath their feet.

So he lay on his stomach in the dappled sunshine by the gently-running stream, one hand on her shoulder, and heard the occasional fly buzz round them, and didn't care, and before he dozed off his mind repeated, 'One Moment in Annihilation's Waste, One Moment, of the Well of Life to taste – The Stars are setting and the Caravan Starts for the Dawn of Nothing – Oh, make haste!' Again he kept the words within his mind because he knew that if she heard them she might make some remark about how caravans and caravan-sites were spoiling not only England but the whole Continent – and that he couldn't stand, no, not even from Mavis.

Unwittingly, he had quoted wise words to himself. He had need to make haste. The Caravan was indeed about to start, if not for the Dawn of Nothing at least for a destination then unknown to him, which was probably just as well.

In the event nothing occurred to spoil that wonderful period with Mavis in Portugal, though once, when the local electricity supply broke down, he and she had had to fumble their way up some unlighted stairs in a restaurant. He could see the glowing ends of the cigarettes of people sitting on the staircase and was glad to get to the top even though nobody said or did anything except to say 'good evening', politely.

CHAPTER 4

The day after their return to London Mavis reminded
him to ring up the features editor of the *Sunday News.*

Thereafter things on the newspaper side moved very
quickly. The £5,000 contract was signed the same day,
a Tuesday, and on the evening of that same day a
Sunday News features man sat in their basement flat and
talked to them while a tape-recorder whirled on a side
table.

At one point the question of the confessional was
raised. Lawrence Brown skittered lightly over the subject,
talking only in general terms, adding that he wished to
clear his mind about certain aspects of this matter.

The *Sunday News* writer did not press the point. He
was a thin, grey-haired man with a bony face, a chain
smoker; unlike his hard grey eyes his voice was soft,
almost gentle. He had said his name was John Bartlet.

Bartlet nodded. But he swung his long thin nose in
Lawrence Brown's direction and said,

'Of course, of course. I understand that. We can leave
it for the moment. Perhaps next week we can – I mean
some time you'll have to—'

He did not finish the sentence. Lawrence Brown
finished it for him.

'Come clean, is that what you were going to say?'

A wintery little smile flickered across Bartlet's face.

'Well – perhaps not quite so bluntly.'

Lawrence Brown nodded, and the subject was dropped.
In the old days, he had heard, there were seaside slot-

machines where you put a coin in and saw a short sequence entitled, 'What the Butler Saw'. Nowadays people would be able to pay their money and read in the *Sunday News* something even better: 'What the Priest Heard'; that and the Mavis saga. The *Sunday News* wasn't paying a large sum for accounts of what it is like to run a Church bazaar.

Before he left Bartlet collected a few photographs and snapshots. Some of Lawrence Brown's early days, as a child, some of his priesthood period, and a selection taken recently in Portugal, and developed and printed with surprising speed by a chemist's shop in Sesimbra.

The preliminary advertising of the articles was due to begin on the Thursday in some national daily newspapers, and in the London evening papers.

He sighed as he closed the door behind Bartlet. He had sold his soul, not to the devil, because he no longer believed in the devil; but he had sold his soul, whatever his soul was; not all of it, just a piece of it, about £5,000 worth, because Mavis had said he should since they needed money.

She had had no need to nag him about it. He knew it well enough. He had inherited a little money from an aunt a year or so before he left the Church, about £3,000; in the nick of time, he thought grimly. She would not have left it to him now.

He had bought a few luxuries for his own bedroom at the presbytery, a decent bedside lamp, a strip of carpet for the linoleum beside his bed, a really comfortable armchair, a portable radio – and the secondhand car, of course, the old Ford Anglia, now on its second engine but it had done 90,000 miles and was still going well on the whole.

All sorts of things had continued to knock a big hole

in the legacy. The honeymoon had been costly and there had been the expense of more furniture and things for Mavis's basement flat in Palace Road, for they had decided that until they could find somewhere else he would move in with her. It was unfortunate that it was within the borders of his previous parish, but it couldn't be helped. Accommodation was in short supply and rents high. He sometimes admitted to himself that it was not a dream love-nest, consisting as it did of a living-room, kitchen and one bedroom. There was a door to the basement steps but access to the house above had been blocked by a wall where formerly a door had led to a staircase. Her cheap modern furniture was showing wear and tear and the light-brown paper and wall paint could be depressing even on a May evening, and it depressed him now.

Many things would be more expensive now that he was no longer a priest. Old Fred Mulliner, of Mulliner's Garage, who sometimes served at Mass, would do most of the repairs to the car himself, and charge nothing for the labour; and very little or nothing for spare parts, because he scrounged around and picked up serviceable secondhand parts; sometimes he alleged they had 'dropped off a lorry'. He himself had never seen these things dropping off lorries but if Fred Mulliner could square his own conscience in some convoluted way it was not for his parish priest to cross-examine him.

Bates, the butcher, had let him have stuff at cost price, and sometimes a joint or a small turkey or a hare for nothing; and there was a cobbler who had never charged anything; and if they all spread the cost thinly over other customers, well, so be it, most of those other customers probably gave little in Church, so it was a kind of rough justice, in a way.

But it would be different now, of course. If he went

and saw them they wouldn't want to know him. And not only the tradesmen.

In the old days it was Father this and Father that, and what shall I do about this, and what do you think about that, Father, and yes, Father, no, Father, three bags full, Father, I agree with you, Father. He would miss the deference, yes, he would, he admitted it to himself. All he had now and would have, for some time, he supposed, was Mavis, and sometimes she said, 'Yes, Larry,' and often she said, 'No, Larry,' and occasionally, 'Not dam' likely,' or even 'Don't be so bloody daft, Larry.'

But she was a great girl, and he didn't regret anything.

John Bartlet of the *Sunday News* worked very hard and very fast, keeping up his strength with cigarettes, cups of strong, sweet red tea, and occasional nips of whisky from a flask.

So that on the Thursday, when the first publicity was appearing, a youngster from the *Sunday News* had already arrived with galley-proofs, as had been agreed; and he waited, now and again glancing rather pointedly at his wristwatch, as Lawrence Brown ran through the proofs and initialled them.

Although he read through them forcedly rather quickly, he felt decidedly uneasy. It was awful by his standards but he felt there was nothing he could do about it now. The first article was appearing on Sunday. The publicity machine was under way. The contract was signed, he had already received £2,000 and there would be a further £1,000 after each article had appeared. A comforting thought was that his bank balance now stood at £2,678 instead of £678.

The third and final of the three articles dealt in detail with the love angle, and was marked at the top SET & HOLD. The first article, dealing with childhood and early days in the priesthood was not too bad, apart from the sickening introduction. It was the second article, dealing with secrets of the confessional, which worried him. This was also marked SET & HOLD. But it was, in fact, only one quarter of an article. John Bartlet had spun out as best he could the harmless generalities provided for him. But the proofs of these finished abruptly, and underneath were the words MORE FOLLOWS, printed in capital letters.

Mavis went out early on the Sunday morning and bought a copy of the newspaper. She thought it was all rather exciting and the article 'super'.

Reading it at breakfast, Lawrence Brown suffered a brief return of his queasiness. The headlines of the feature article had been the first shock because he hadn't realised that when in print the whole thing would look as bad as it did. The main headline across the front page was about an inch high: FATHER BROWN'S OWN STORY.

A smaller headline read: The Priest Who Got Away From It All Tells The Facts. The introduction said:

Today the *Sunday News* tells the story the world has been awaiting, of the Roman Catholic priest who decided to break the bonds of priesthood and renounce his vows for the sake of the woman he loved.

Up to now Father Brown has been silent. Now he has decided to tell all, the whole amazing story of how he braved the fury of the Catholic hierarchy for the sake of Mavis Bailey, a waitress in a small restaurant where sometimes, weary from tramping on his rounds visiting the sick, he would pop in for a pot of tea and a slice of toast.

He tells how she came to him in her marital distress,

how love developed, how they planned secretly, until at last they faced reality together.

No longer a priest, a self-admitted atheist, he reveals some of the secrets of the confessional, being no longer bound by the rules imposing secrecy on a priest.

It is a story of passion in the parish, of loves and hates, the illegal goings-on of a Member of Parliament, a Councillor's fiddles, a gangster's crimes, told exclusively to the *Sunday News*.

There was a single-column picture of himself at the church door after some wedding ceremony he had long forgotten, a single-column picture of an old studio portrait of Mavis, and a big blown-up snap of himself and Mavis on a beach in Portugal on their honeymoon. They were both in swimsuits. He was, at any rate, and he had to admit that he looked rather good in bathing trunks; long legs, broad shouldered, suntanned, dark, muscular. Mavis was in her old bikini, smiling at him in what she imagined to be a loving way, though, to be frank, he thought she looked rather soppy. She was showing the curves of her thighs and bosom. It was one of her favourite snaps.

She must have given it to Bartlet when he asked for pictures. He himself wouldn't have given it to him. It unveiled a good deal of the story, just as it revealed much of her body.

He recalled the proof headlines of the second article:

CONFESSIONAL!
Father Brown Reveals Amazing Things Well Known Men And Women Whispered To Him

And the final one, of course, told how he met and fell in love with Mavis. He flushed as he remembered the headlines on the proofs:

SEX IN THE PARISH
How I Loved And Left

There was a detailed description of the honeymoon in Portugal and more revealing snapshots of Mavis in swimsuits, and one of him eating breakfast in his dressing-gown on the balcony of a hotel. The caption was hideous: AFTER ANOTHER NIGHT OF LOVE – FATHER BROWN, IN HIS NEW FOUND HAPPINESS, ENJOYS COFFEE AND ROLLS IN THE SUNSHINE.

He had thought of pointing out to the newspaper that although he was drinking coffee he wasn't rolling in the sunshine. And he had not been weary on his feet when he had called at the New Speranza. He had been driving on his rounds in his car, and he hadn't consumed toast and drunk tea. He'd always had coffee and a scone. But he had let it all go. What was the use of protesting? You didn't get £5,000 for being tetchy about details.

He'd mentioned to Bartlet how much he admired the *Rubáiyát* and he noted they'd even dragged that in, making him say in the very first passage of the first article, 'Omar Khayyám frequently implies in his verses in the *Rubáiyát* how he found solace for his own agnosticism in wine. He fell in love with wine. If you read the *Rubáiyát* and substitute Love for Wine you will understand a little of how I felt – and feel. I fell out of love with my faith, and I fell in love with Love. All right, sex, if you like.'

They had to drag sex in, of course, spell it out in detail, in case anybody didn't see what they were getting at. It was all right for them. But it was his name on the articles.

The series had been well advertised in advance. And there had been ordinary straight news stories when he left the Church. His name, with its implied connotations

44

with Chesterton's priest, was itself eye-catching. And he had expected a letter of protest from his former bishop about the articles, perhaps even from the Cardinal himself. But there had been none. No phone call, either. Nothing. Blank silence.

When he had left the Church he had written a letter to his Bishop, with a carbon-copy to the Cardinal, explaining his reasons, and posted them before leaving for Portugal.

The Bishop had replied with a punctilious little note; 'I have received your letter of farewell and note that you now have other calls upon your time.' That was all. From the Cardinal had come a carbon-copy of the letter the Cardinal had sent to the Bishop.

Among a number of paragraphs dealing with purely administrative matters there was only one brief reference to him: 'I note that Father Lawrence Brown has decided to go his own way. (In the vernacular I understand this is known as Doing Your Own Thing.) Pity. There was good material there somewhere.' That was all.

So that now, although he disliked the morning post forwarded from the presbytery, it was not because he feared a kick-back from the hierarchy but rather from former colleagues at a low level, or from disillusioned parishioners. Yet there again there had been nothing; most of the letters were for Mavis, usually anonymous, mostly abusive and sometimes outright obscene. She had agreed to let him open any letters addressed to her when she did not recognise the probable sender.

He himself, after the first two or three, did not bother to read them to the end before tearing them up. The opening three or four words were enough. Apart from the obvious ones such as 'harlot' or 'cheap tart', there was the usual sprinkling of four-letter words, the whole normally printed in block letters, posted locally, and supposedly unidentifiable, though he could have made a good guess at the names of one or two of the senders if he'd tried.

In his heart, he was surprised by what he supposed he should call the Church's angry silence, if indeed it was angry, and not merely an indifferent silence. The cool attitude of the Cardinal and his Bishop he found, in fact, rather unfair if not downright hurtful. He had, after all, worked hard during his six years in the parish until he met Mavis and, though he said it himself, had done quite well. He was a good preacher. People had sometimes come from other parishes to listen to him, and some of his better passages had been printed verbatim in the local papers.

Admittedly the *Sunday News* had hammed it all up, but the fact remained that what he had done was dramatic. And if newspaper men and doubtless many ordinary citizens could see this, one might expect one's former Church superiors and colleagues to take the same view. He told himself that he was not annoyed, just surprised, that was all.

On the evening of the Sunday when the first article appeared he sat down in the armchair by the grate in the living-room and leaned his head against the chairback, thinking he could do that safely because he had not put any oil on his hair that morning. Mavis got scratchy in her practical, north-country way if he soiled the back of the chair with hair oil.

Out in the kitchen the drip of the kitchen tap as the water fell into the washing-up basin reminded him that he had promised her to put some 'smalls' to soak in a bucket. 'Come, fill the Cup, and in the Fire of Spring The Winter Garment of Repentance fling,' he thought. He also thought, 'The Bird of Time has but a little way To fly – and Lo! the Bird is on the Wing,' and he knew

46

one bird who would soon be on the wing, and that was Mavis on the way back from the pub. Nappies, as distinct from baby clothes, were done by the nappy service people, though he had to change the baby now and then, and that was bad enough.

Mavis would not be interested in 'Winter Garments of Repentance', but she'd expect to see other garments put in to soak. There would be no baby garments for another two weeks, thank goodness. The baby was called Rod, for some reason, and had gone to stay with Mavis's mother in Newcastle while they were in Portugal, and wasn't back yet.

Beyond knowing that he wasn't the father of this baby he knew little about it, and Mavis had been what he could only call shifty when questioned.

She had told some garbled story of an association which hadn't worked out, and when he pressed for further details had tossed her blonde head and said, 'Love me, love my baby,' and looked at him defiantly, and said no more. Nor had he.

In the infatuated mood he was in he decided that if some French king had believed that 'Paris is well worth a Mass,' then 'Mavis is well worth a baby.' But he knew he would return to the matter one day.

As it turned out Mavis was not so soon on the wing as he expected. He knew the Sportsman's Bowl didn't open till seven o'clock on Sundays but it was now a quarter to nine. He began to think again about the confession article. He had a date with Bartlet for Tuesday evening but he would put him off till Wednesday evening, perhaps even Thursday morning. Bartlet wouldn't like it but he was a fast worker. He could cope, and it would give more time to ponder.

Now he heard the basement door slam and knew that Mavis was back, and a few seconds later she swirled into the room, wearing her grey slacks and light-blue blouse, and flung her arms round his neck.

'Hello, Larry, hinny – missed me?'

'As always,' he murmured, kissing her, pushing back her blonde hair, looking at her with eyes of love. 'Bit late, aren't you?'

He didn't go to the pub much himself because people were inclined to stop talking and stare at him and whisper when he came in. They did the same when Mavis went in alone, she said, but she didn't seem to care. He knew she had friends from the old days, that life in the basement flat was dull for her, and he was really quite glad that she went there for an hour or so in the early evening. She deserved a little light-hearted fun and she never drank too much, and was always back to cook his supper, not that she was much of a cook. She was too impatient, but the food was no worse than that at the presbytery.

Tonight she was much later than usual, but he did not mention it again.

'See anybody you knew?' he asked.

'Only Ron Flint and the boys. I've bought a new car, that's why I'm late.'

He stared at her, shocked and even horrified.

'New car?'

She nodded happily. 'The old Anglia's had it, hinny. You know that.'

'Yes, but – the cost.'

'It's not a new – new car. Secondhand, really, but as good as new. Rover—'

'How much?' he murmured.

'Only seventeen hundred—'

'Seventeen hundred!'

She looked at him reproachfully.

'I thought you'd be pleased! Ron's getting it for me.

We can pay by instalments, and Ron's fixing it so that we don't have to pay interest, see? Ron knows people. Owner has had to go abroad – suddenly. Anyway, there's the *Sunday News* money.'

Lawrence Brown forgot all about the new car and the new financial commitment. For some time it had been Ron this and Ron that and Ron the other. He had only met a Ron once, and that was some years previously. But Ron, if it was the same one, was part of his current problem. Ron was one of the little group who seemed to creep out of the shadows sometimes to gather round his bed and frighten him in the darkness of the early morning hours. Not the chief menace perhaps, but a nasty, vicious one if he hadn't reformed.

Quite suddenly he knew he was going to have a confrontation with Mavis. He almost welcomed it, as a man might feel as he settles into a dentist's chair to have a tooth out. There was no escape.

'Can I ask you something personal, Mavis?'

'We should have no secrets, Larry, love.'

'Have you had an affaire with Ron – in the past, of course?'

She laughed. 'Affaire? Crummy old-fashioned word, that is!'

'I am old-fashioned still – in some ways.'

'You could have kidded *me*,' she said, and knew from his expression that he enjoyed the flattery. She looked him in the face:

'Yes, I was keen on him, since you ask.'

'Why?'

'Sex,' she said simply. 'Then suddenly he was a near-killer, first a burglar, then a near-killer, see? It kind of shocked me at the time. He did a warehouse, but he got disturbed by an old night-watchman, and he just wanted to thump the bloke, knock him out, see, but the bloke fought back and Ron thumped him too hard and nearly killed him, and I didn't like that. Why didn't you ask all this before we...?'

He looked at her steadily. He was sure now that it was the same Ron as the one who had confessed to lots of things when he thought there was a chance he might die – things such as thumping a night-watchman too hard. He was tempted, almost beyond endurance, to tell Mavis. But Ron was part of his unsolved problem. Later, perhaps. Not now.

'Because I loved you as you were, and still do.'

'Dear old Larry!'

'Anybody after Ron?'

'Chap called Duncan,' she said abruptly.

'Duncan?'

'Ron was doing a year or two in Wandsworth prison. I was getting on a bit. Duncan was a nice guy. Had a good regular job. Kind of generous. But then I met Ron again – after he came out. Met him a couple of times a month. Maybe more.'

'Why? Why, if you were married to – Duncan?'

She looked at him astonished at his naïvety.

'I wasn't *married* to him – just shacked up with him. Like with you, love. He was a real good guy, was Duncan, but he wasn't no good at love, not like you, Larry lad, you're good, Larry, now you've got the hang of it. You're good for me.'

He should have left it at that. He should have been almost pleased and reassured in a way, and left it at that. The past was the past. But he wanted to force full details from her, to have the jealous pain all at one go. Then he would put it all from him.

'When you were shacked up with Duncan – where?'

'Where? Here, of course.'

Lawrence Brown cleared his throat and asked a final

question, though he feared he knew the answer already.

'And Ron? How did you meet him while you were still – shacked up with Duncan?'

She laughed.

'Bit nosy, aren't you? Duncan had his nine-to-five job. And I had a few hours off in the day, being a waitress, as you know – as you ought to know,' she replied brightly, and if she had been sitting beside him he was sure she would have nudged him in the ribs. 'And Ron's time was his own, him being still a burglar in those days. So we had a snack – and so on. Dead easy. Couldn't go wrong.'

'Where?'

'Here, of course, where else? Everybody else in the house was out at work except an old doll on the top floor and she's room-bound. Dead easy.'

He stared at her and felt the blood mounting in his face.

'Here? In our bed?'

She shook her head impatiently.

'Look, hinny, if you worry about who's slept or died in what bed you'll never buy a secondhand bed or stay in a hotel, will you? Still love me?'

She pulled his head down and kissed him on the lips, and he felt the old magic sweep through his bloodstream.

'Always will,' he said softly.

'Whey, ye boogger,' she responded happily, and released him. 'Now I'll go and fry up the fish.' She went out to the kitchen humming to herself.

While she was cooking, Lawrence Brown pulled a letter out of his pocket and stared at it, thinking of the cost of a new car and the fact that he hadn't yet found a regular job. The *Sunday News* money wouldn't last for ever. At first he had hoped to become a religious correspondent or general adviser on a Church of England or a Methodist publication and had written several hopeful letters, but there had been no response. Not even a letter of acknowledgement, which he considered very bad manners.

He looked at the letter again. It was vaguely worded, was not from any of the publications to which he had written, and he had taken little notice of it when it had arrived that morning.

The writing paper was headed: Catholic & General Publishing Company Ltd., 334 Poland Street, London W.1., and read:

Dear Father Brown (if I may so address you),
It occurs to me that a short talk might be of mutual interest. I would be happy to see you almost any afternoon, this week, at about 3 p.m., if you would care to call. Perhaps you would kindly ring my secretary if you are agreeable.

Yours sincerely,
Ernest Markham
(Managing Director)

He assumed they wished to get him to review some controversial book, perhaps, or write a foreword for it. If so, it would be better than nothing. It would occupy an hour or two, though he was not interested in controversy. He only wanted peace, a quiet life, and Mavis. Nevertheless he made up his mind to telephone the following morning, and perhaps call in the afternoon.

As he lay awake in bed that night some of the old fear came back. There was one confession in particular which was at the root of his apprehension. And with the fear came the twinges of conscience, creeping out of the darkness of the room, worrying at him as a dog worries a ham-bone.

He had heard the worrying confession under the seal

of the confessional. Now he was no longer bound religiously by that seal. If he were now bound by anything the bonds were those of a citizen whose duty in certain matters differed considerably from that of a priest. A priest could persuade and console and withhold absolution. But he couldn't divulge. The old arguments and theories again went round and round in his sleepless mind. An ordinary citizen, no longer a priest, could and probably would divulge.

Others besides himself would be thinking that.

That was the whole trouble; others besides himself would be thinking as he was. And they would hunt him down. He was in no doubt about it. He was surprised they had not done so already. Or were they just preparing? Was the train of events which must end in his death already under way? There had been one or two little incidents even while he and Mavis were in Portugal which had made him uneasy, not to say fearful.

He didn't think he had long to live.

The bird of time had but a little way to fly, he was convinced of that; and the bird was already on the wing, he was also convinced of that.

He put out his hand and stroked Mavis.

He had told her nothing of his fears. She wouldn't understand, thinking that such things don't happen in Britain. But he was sure they did.

CHAPTER 5

Poland Street lies on the edge of Soho as if it were a link between the underwear of Oxford Street and the underworld of strip-clubs and clip-joints.

A few eighteenth-century terraced houses still remain, like relics of the housing boom of the 1780s, but they and their nineteenth-century equivalents are interspersed with modern buildings, giving them an air of shabby survivors.

The whole street is a jumble of people wanting to sell anything from pins and buttons to dresses (strictly wholesale). Some of the houses display a number of boards – model agencies, photographers and small workshops here live on the edge of hope. On the corner of the street two Sikhs in snow-white turbans chattered excitedly of some convoluted business deal.

The larger modern buildings, occupying two or three sites, with their modern plate-glass windows, speak of the prosperous, those who started in the basement and worked up; while the small hopeful cards and boards announce the barely surviving ones, or perhaps those about to disappear. One day they have hope, a basement, a letterhead, and the next their place is occupied by a 'To let' sign.

He had taken the Underground to Oxford Circus and trudged along Great Marlborough Street to Poland Street and turned right. He had put on his new dark-blue suit, a white shirt and red tie, and wore his three-quarter-length hound's-tooth shower-proof overcoat in case it rained. It was raining now, and he put up his umbrella.

He had polished his shoes, black ones with elastic at the sides, a relic from his priesthood days but in very good condition, real leather, sold to him at a cheap price by the cobbler who used to mend his shoes free. The rain would dull the shining toe-caps but it couldn't be helped. He had done his best to look smart and had arrived fifteen minutes too early, as people will for an important appointment.

To fill in the time he wandered round nearby Berwick Market, listening to the hubbub of voices and peering at the fruit and vegetable stalls and the rows of cheap clothing, piles of crockery and rows of necklaces. Although many things were for sale, the pervading smell was of fruit and vegetables.

Here was one of the few remaining scenes of bustling London Cockney enterprise and cheerfulness. He made a mental note to buy some oranges for Mavis, who was always moaning about the price of them, after his meeting with Mr Ernest Markham. It wouldn't do to arrive carrying a paper bag full of oranges; just as it wouldn't do to arrive too early, because it looked as though you were too keen.

If asked to describe what he imagined about the building he was to visit, he would have said it was probably an elegantly-shaped narrow building, with touches of stucco here and there. But inside there would be mellow wood panelling, wall-to-wall carpeting, with an occasional rubber plant. He might be met by a smart, slick cookie of a receptionist, who would hand him on to a thin, cultured secretary with an intense, sensitive, pale face.

C. & G. House was narrow, devoid of stucco, coloured grey, and in need of repainting. It was occupied by several different firms, but inside the shabby hall a notice on the wall said C. & G. Publishing Co., 2nd Floor, and a hand with a drooping forefinger pointed up the dusty, uncarpeted stairs.

He was not discouraged. On the contrary, he felt a vague, pleasurable sensation because there was an aura of almost Dickensian decay about it all. He had an idea that Mr Markham would sign his contract with a quill pen in a room totally different from the rest of the building, and then dry it with sand.

A plump girl behind a window on the second floor said, 'Yeah?'

'I have an appointment with Mr Markham,' he said mildly.

'Name?'

'Brown – *Father* Brown, I used to be.'

She looked at a desk diary and then up at him, and he was pleased to note what seemed to be a faint flicker of interest in her pudding face. She pressed a buzzer and said,

'Down the corridor. Third door on the right.'

He had a sort of feeling that in a firm like the Catholic & General Publishing Company she might at least have called him 'Mr' or even given him the courtesy title of Father, not that it mattered. It was different in the old days but he was getting used to things.

At the third door down the corridor the scene did indeed change. He was met at the door by a young woman who was tall, slim, pale, as he had imagined a publisher's secretary would be, with thick black hair tied with a dark-blue ribbon on the nape of her neck, big grey eyes, an oval face and broad, smooth forehead. The ribbon was the same colour as the thick carpet of her room.

To the left as he entered he saw through a half-opened door an extension of the carpet, panelling on the wall, rows of books with different coloured jackets and the corner of what was obviously a massive mahogany desk.

'Mr Markham will see you now,' she murmured, stood aside so that he could go through the communicating door, and softly closed it behind him.

The name Ernest Markham meant nothing to him, except that he dimly recalled that in the little garden behind the presbytery there was a clematis called Ernest Markham.

He imagined Ernest Markham as perhaps a quiet, scholarly man, with grey hair and smouldering eyes with dark shadows under them, a thinker, dedicated to publishing the truth in all its multiple aspects.

Once in the room he noticed a rich smell of cigar-smoke mingled with toilet-water, and Mr Ernest Markham rose and came forward from behind his desk with outstretched hand. He bore no resemblance to a clematis. He wore a near-black suit with a broad white pinstripe, a pink shirt and a light-blue plain tie. That was all that Father Brown noticed at first glance, except that Mr Markham was of only medium height and must have weighed about sixteen or seventeen stones.

But when he came forward to shake hands he did not waddle. His steps were short and purposeful, and his hand, though large and white and soft, produced a strong handshake. He motioned Lawrence Brown to sit in a low armchair by the side of his desk.

'Drink, Father?'

'No, thanks, bit early for me.'

'Not too early for me,' said Ernest Markham, giving a slight laugh which sounded like 'yuck-yuck', and moving to a corner cupboard where he kept his drinks. The key had fallen to the carpet and he bent down to pick it up. Lawrence Brown thought he had never seen such a massive posterior encased in trousers with such short legs.

The publisher poured himself out a strong whisky, added a splash of soda, sat down, swivelled his chair so that he was looking down on his visitor, and pushed a cedar-wood box towards him.

'Cigar?'

'Mind if I smoke a pipe?'

Mr Markham waved a hand.

'Smoke what you like, when you like, how you like. In here, that is. My wife Rachael, she don't mind cigars or cigarettes, but she don't like pipes, not in her office.' Again he waved his hand, this time towards the room next door and the slim woman in it. Lawrence Brown tried not to look surprised.

'Your wife is your secretary?'

'Sure she is. I pay her good money. Wife-as-secretary. Good for income, good for tax. Get it?'

He winked and laughed. This time there were three yucks. He spoke in a deep, rich voice, with a mixture of occasional American words and expressions and a general faint Cockney undertone.

Lawrence Brown looked at him more closely, particularly his face, and his impressions were strangely mixed; as, later, they were to be mixed in his mind about his whole relationship with Ernest Markham.

The facial skin was sallow. That meant nothing. A German artist had told him, 'People are born with a skin of a certain colour. They can modify it by sun-bathing or other means, but the basic colour of the skin is what they were born with.'

It was a big face to match his thick neck and broad shoulders. And he was bald down to the tips of his ears on either side. His eyes were dark brown and, at the moment, glistened benevolently.

It was the eyebrows which fascinated Father Brown. They were dark, the same colour as the eyes, but crescent shaped, stretching from the sides of the eyes in a wide curve until they almost met above his broad, fleshy nose. There was nothing remarkable about the chin or jaw-line and underneath, as might have been expected, were a few extra chins – two or three, depending on how he held his head.

Now, as Markham looked at his visitor and smiled, he resembled, if not a kindly Buddha, at least a tolerant but alert oriental magnate of mixed blood. Father Brown thought that as it was clearly impossible that the clematis, Ernest Markham, should have been named after him, then he himself must have adopted the name after the clematis. Not that it mattered.

Ernest Markham took a gulp of whisky, half empty-ing the glass, and said,

'Well now, Father Brown, what can I do for you?'

Lawrence Brown wasn't going to wear that one. His training in logic saw the trap. He said gently,

'Isn't that the wrong way round, Mr Markham?'

For a second the smile died out of the oriental eyes.

'Meaning?'

'Meaning nothing. Just that *you* wrote to *me*, suggest-ing I call sometime. So, just setting the scene, what can *I* do for *you*?'

'Or what can we do for each other?'

'Maybe. What can we?'

'Make money,' said Ernest Markham, and smiled broadly so that the ends of his lips reached upwards towards the outer ends of his eyebrows. 'Just that – make money, big money. You need it, I like it. Correct?'

Lawrence Brown thought it out, then he said, 'I can't speak for *you*, Mr Markham.'

'Speak for yourself.'

'I don't need it.'

'Not now, thanks to the *Sunday News*. But you will.

59

Later. Maybe when it's too late, when – if I may say so – you will no longer be of much interest. Gather ye rosebuds, and capital, while ye may, Father!'

Ernest Markham's face creased again. He sat back in his chair and gave a four-yuck laugh.

He spoke unpalatable truths, yet Lawrence Brown couldn't dislike him, not then, not at that moment.

'You want a book, I suppose, by me?' he asked.

'That's the rough idea.'

Lawrence Brown nodded. Then he shook his head dismally.

'Apart from anything else, it's all been published – or will be.'

Ernest Markham smiled. 'All? In three instalments?' Markham said. 'In three instalments in a Sunday newspaper? All? Shall I tell you something?'

'If you like.'

'Few things sell better than a book by—' He stopped.

'By?' Lawrence Brown guessed what was coming, braced himself for it, to hear it spelt out, C-A-T spells cat.

'By a renegade priest,' said Ernest Markham flatly. Although he had expected it, Lawrence Brown blinked.

'Except, of course, a book by a renegade nun,' Markham added. 'And they're a bit thin on the ground, ain't they? Well, ain't they? You don't pick renegade nuns up so easy, do you? In short supply, that's what nuns are these days.'

He smiled so that once again the absurdly small rosy mouth split and his lips spread across his face like a slice of water-melon.

'Don't forget the song old Wolfie Mankowitz wrote, "Nothin' is for nothin', nothin' is for free, I look after you, boy, you look after me." Great little song. That's life, boy, you don't know it, you led a sheltered life, you did. Soon you'll be getting down to the nitty-gritty, you

60

will. So I look after you, boy, you look after me, right?'

'What sort of book?'

Ernest Markham turned his big round face upwards and gazed at the ceiling, his liquid brown eyes thoughtful, then he turned to Father Brown and the ex-priest noted again the complete baldness of the man's head down to an inch or so above his ears. He had raised his thin eyebrows, and the crescent shape of them was paralleled by the lines on his forehead. He looked like a thoughtful, kindly owl.

'It's like this,' he said. 'As a start the book'll be roughly the same as the newspaper stuff, see? A quick run-up, you know, early childhood, and some flam about your old mom, then the priesthood stuff, caged eagle, pinioned, all that, straining to be free, to soar with strong wings into the upper atmosphere of liberated thought. But we keep that short, see? Just background, see?

'Then on to the bulk of the book – what you heard in the confessional – and in some detail, more than the *Sunday News* stuff. Then a nice long bit about you and the lady – I don't want no tortured conscience stuff, just facts, what happened *before* you did a bunk with her, how and when, and then a few practical facts about the first night of your honeymoon and all that. Or whenever you first made love to her, you being a priest and not knowing much about—'

'Yes, I understand.'

'Yeah?'

'Pornography, really, disguised pornography, isn't it?'

Mr Markham banged the top of his massive desk with a big, strong fist. He seemed genuinely outraged. He said,

'Porn – no, it ain't porn! Porn don't do the firm no good! Not in the long run, porn don't. Porn's okay for a quick killing, see, but it don't do the firm no good in the long run!'

He got up and began to stump up and down the room with his quick, decided little steps, white hands clasped behind his near-black jacket with its broad white pinstripe.

'Porn leads to trouble in the end,' Mr Markham muttered. 'What's more, it ain't moral, see? We don't go in for no porn, but facts is truth, and truth is beautiful, ain't it?'

He stopped and stared at his visitor and shook his head solemnly so that two and a half chins wobbled.

'You got to understand that, mister – truth is beautiful – otherwise you won't write proper. You got to hold nothing back, otherwise you won't be sincere, you won't.'

Lawrence Brown had got up out of his chair so that he did not need to talk over his shoulder. He said,

'I do understand what you want, but you are a Catholic publishing house, and it seems odd to me—'

Ernest Markham stopped stumping backwards and forwards. He came up to his visitor and stood in front of him and prodded him in the midriff and said,

'You got it wrong, you have, the name is Catholic *and General*, okay? Sure we publish Catholic stuff – you got a new line on the Pope, we'll publish it; you want a cheap Catechism, we'll quote you real good terms, same for new paperback missals. New ideas on the Talmud or the Torah – we're interested, got a friend who wants to be a guru and has a few followers, okay, we'll knock out some pamphlets, know what?'

Mr Markham prodded him again.

'Tell you something. This firm was going bust when I took over. Know what I did? "Do me a favour," I said, "less of the Catholic, more of the General. Nothing subversive, mind you. No Commie or Fascist stuff, and no porn – not real porn, it don't do the firm no good,"

62

that's what I said. Never looked back. Ten per cent dividends last year – before tax, of course.'

Lawrence Brown shook his head slowly and said, 'It's not really my scene, to use a common expression.'

Ernest Markham looked at him and agitated his jowls.

'How do you see your scene?' he asked softly. 'What about the nitty-gritty? Bread-and-butter, wife, kid, all that? Now this book of yours—'

'There is no book of mine.'

Ernest Markham ignored the interruption.

'Hardback, paperback, world sales – America, France, Germany, Sweden, Denmark, Holland, Italy, South America, Japan, radio, television, film rights—'

'No book of that kind because—'

Ernest Markham cut him short.

'You want to watch it, you do. You with a wife and kid.'

How did he know about the baby? So far there had been no mention of the child in the *Sunday News*. He'd done his homework well.

'You want to watch it,' he said again. 'Money don't last long these days, not after tax. You've been sheltered, you don't know about these things. I'm sorry for you, really sorry I am, 'cos if you don't watch it you're going to be in need of care and attention.'

Lawrence Brown reached for his umbrella.

'Tell you what I'll do,' said Ernest Markham suddenly. 'I'll make it a package-deal. I like you, you're intelligent, you got brains, you got a good personality.'

'Package-deal?'

Ernest Markham had widened his rosebud mouth again. His brown, near-oriental eyes under the crescent eyebrows were soft and liquid. He said,

'We publish the book. Good publicity. We all make

63

cash. And in addition – you want to think about this – in addition you join the firm, see? Theological adviser or something. We get a lot of tripe in here. You flip through it, see if there's anything worth having. Commercially, that is.'

He tapped his teeth with a gold pencil and said,

'Three thousand pounds a year to start. One year's contract, see how it works out. If it does, maybe you join the Board, maybe become a director. Maybe a job for life, pension, all that. Four weeks' holiday,' he added as an afterthought, 'same as me.'

Lawrence Brown put down his umbrella on a side table. Ernest Markham said quickly,

'Think about it. We'll see you are all right, boy.'

'I have done.'

He was repeating mentally the lines of Omar Khayyám: ' "How sweet is mortal Sovranty!" – think some: Others – "How blest the Paradise to come!" Ah, take the cash in hand and waive the rest; Oh, the brave Music of a *distant* Drum!' He nodded and said,

'All right, Mr Markham. I agree.' He'd take the cash.

'You've cut yourself in on a gold mine,' said Ernest Markham. 'That's what you've done, cut yourself in on a gold mine.'

His cigar had gone out. He lit a match and held it to the end of the cigar, preparatory to relighting it. He said,

'I'll get a paragraph or two into some gossip columns.'

He began to pace up and down again, hands behind his back, speaking about the paragraphs he already saw in print. 'Father Brown's forthcoming book is likely to cause some heart-searching. More than one public person among M.P.s, town councillors and even criminal circles is believed to be sleeping uneasily. What will Father Brown reveal about the confessions he has heard during

64

his priesthood? That is what is worrying them. Many people will guess where and whom the caps will fit. In his crusade to clean up public life Father Brown will go into details of cases at which he only hinted in his recent newspaper articles.

'"I feel it my duty to strike this blow for decency," Father Brown told my reporter. "The public has suffered long enough from this canker in our midst."'

Markham stopped.

As Lawrence Brown listened his heart sank to a new low. This was his death warrant. He did not know who would execute the warrant, or how. He only knew that he was doomed.

'I want a good advance – ten thousand pounds,' he said sharply. 'And I want it before that stuff goes into the gossip columns.'

Even extravagant little Mavis could carry on for a while with £10,000; especially if Ron Flint was there to advise her, he thought bitterly.

Ernest Markham looked at his gold wristwatch.

'We'll discuss it some other time, Father. And now, if you'll excuse me, I have another appointment.'

He began to shuffle with some papers on his desk.

'We'll discuss it tomorrow,' said Lawrence Brown. 'I will call at the same time.'

'As you wish,' Ernest Markham said, without looking up. 'Goodbye.'

'Goodbye till tomorrow.'

'You can go out by this other door, it leads to the street.'

'It doesn't matter.'

He was curious to have another look at the svelte young woman whom Markham claimed to be his wife. He didn't believe for a moment that she was his wife.

Yet she didn't look the type who, to use Mavis's words, would *shack up* with a gross creature like Markham.

As he opened the door to leave the room he heard Markham speak behind him,

'Don't push your luck too far, buster.'

He did not reply, but he had a slight nostalgic status-twinge. In the old days nobody would have dared to call Father Lawrence Brown 'buster'.

The impression made by Poland Street depends upon your mood. If you are in a depressed mood, it looks seedy and dirty. If you are in a good mood it seems colourful and lively.

As he made his way along to Berwick Market to buy the oranges for Mavis it seemed to Lawrence Brown a very jolly, carefree street. His own mood had soon lightened to such an extent that life now looked good indeed. He would fiddle the book somehow so as not to say too much, not to put himself in greater peril, if peril there were. There was in prospect just the kind of job he wanted, and although he had mentioned £10,000 as an advance on royalties he would settle for £5,000. And he quoted to himself, ' "Folks of a surly Tapster tell, And daub his Visage with the Smoke of Hell; They talk of some strict Testing of us – Pish! He's a Good Fellow, and 'twill all be well." ' Ernest Markham was a good fellow and 'twill all be well, everybody was a good fellow and the things he had imagined didn't happen in this country.

As he made his way to the Underground station Lawrence Brown in his innocence hummed a little hum to himself like Pooh Bear, and he was humming as he pushed open the door of the basement flat and saw Mavis there to greet him, and he told her the good news and watched her eyes shine.

But at two o'clock in the morning the shadows crept out of the corners of the room once more and stood round the bed gazing down at him speculatively.

CHAPTER 6

When he called on Ernest Markham the following day and heard his opening words Lawrence Brown at first could hardly believe he was hearing right. He had thought everything was as good as buttoned up but Ernest Markham stared at him with his liquid, oriental-looking eyes and said,

'Been speaking to my fellow directors, Father. There's no question of ten thousand pounds' advance on royalties. That's out.'

'I would accept a little less,' he said cautiously. Markham shook his head sadly.

'My fellow directors, they're a bit careful, see? There won't be no royalties at all till you've done a full synopsis of the book, three sample chapters, too, get it?'

'None at all till then? But—'

'That's the form, Father. Don't do no good to argue. Take it or leave it. Ties up a lot of capital, bringing out a book does.'

'And the job you mentioned – religious adviser or something?'

'Depends, doesn't it? I said it depends, doesn't it?'

'On what?' asked Lawrence Brown, and found himself flushing and recognised the danger signal. He had a quick temper and knew it, and people in the parish had known it because once he had lost his temper with Father Davidson in public and once, unpardonably, with an elderly parishioner at an annual bazaar.

Now he felt himself trembling as he fought to control his tongue.

'Depends on what?' he asked loudly, angrily. 'Depends on what?'

'Things. Like whether your face fits. From where I'm sitting, I'm wondering. And something else.'

'What else?' he asked. 'Tell me what else. Yesterday you—'

He was shouting now, and abruptly pulled himself together and did not finish the sentence.

'You don't want to get naughty,' Ernest Markham said mildly. 'It don't help nobody. Depends on if the book's a success, of course. Adds to your reputation – such as it is,' he added thoughtfully. 'We got to get a good foreword from some public figure, see? Make it sound respectable, sort of social document, in a way. Get it?'

Markham didn't wait for an answer. He went on.

'I been in touch with Mr Edward Mallow, he's your M.P. in case you didn't know it.'

Lawrence Brown sat very still and quiet. He did indeed know it.

'He's not so keen,' Markham said. 'I telephoned him, I said you'd go along and talk it over with him, maybe this evening, around nine o'clock, O.K.? Maybe you can talk him into things.'

'I can talk him into doing a foreword, I can talk him into it,' Lawrence Brown said decisively. 'If it's the last thing I do I'll talk him into it.'

'That's my boy,' Markham said approvingly. 'Maybe your face'll fit after all. His address is Flat 3, 213 Eaton Terrace, near Sloane Square.'

He got up and let Lawrence Brown out by a door which led down to the street by the back staircase, and Lawrence Brown, meandering along Poland Street, wondered how to fill in the time until his appointment with

69

Mallow. Eventually he went home to his basement flat.

Mavis was not there. He didn't expect her to be. She would be out shopping, then she would pop into the Sportsman's Bowl for a drink, then she would return and cook his supper. He knew the routine.

He fried himself some bacon and a couple of eggs and ate an early supper, and left her a note saying he had eaten and had to go and see an M.P. in connection with the book. He would be back before midnight.

Then he took an Underground train to Sloane Square, arriving, as usual, fifteen minutes too early for an appointment. He spent the time walking up and down the street rehearsing his approach to Mr Mallow, M.P. Not that it needed much rehearsing. He knew exactly what the form would be.

First he would try persuasion. If that failed it would be too bad. Too bad for Mallow, to be precise. Certain things were permissible in law but unacceptable to public opinion in general. Other things were plain criminal.

Lawrence Brown, who had once heard Mallow's longest confession, knew he had two weapons, either of which could smash his career in Parliament or even in business circles. He was prepared to use either weapon.

Both, in fact, if it were necessary.

It was a warm night for May and he carried his light, hound's-tooth raincoat draped over his left arm. He was very proud of it and knew that it suited his slim figure when he wore it.

He had long since shaved off his beard in response to Mavis's urging. He had done so reluctantly, because he still treasured the mental image he had of himself at the end of the last Mass which he had said; tall, dark-haired, bearded, and almost Christ-like, standing so resolutely there while some scruffy religious fanatic had flung an egg and a tomato at him, and he had heard the rustle and murmuring of the congregation, half caused by a feeling of indignation and outrage but half, he felt sure, in admiration of the man they still thought of as their priest.

He looked at his watch. It showed five minutes to the hour. He turned round and walked back to number 213.

The house had been divided into four flats, one above the other. There was a lift but the house had not been completely modernised in that, although the flat occupants had their names neatly printed on a polished board in the entrance, there was no entry-'phone apparatus. The double swing doors were open for anybody to enter from the street. He noted that Mallow's flat was on the third floor, walked along the carpeted hall to the lift but decided against using it, since walking upstairs would use up the remaining two minutes to his appointment time.

On the second-floor landing he paused for a moment by the lift-gate. The lift had also not been modernised. There was an old-fashioned, grid-type, landing-gate, and as he heard the lift grinding and shuddering its way from above he wondered fleetingly if it was one of the really vintage ones, with a porter who pulled on a rope inside to set it in motion and who slowed it down by hand, too, when it reached its destination.

But there he did the lift an injustice.

Admittedly there was a sliding grid door but it must have been button-operated because there was no porter in uniform inside. It passed him slowly and majestically on its way to the ground floor.

There were two people in the lift, a man in a grey coat at the back partly obscured by a woman he recognised and who recognised him. Ernest Markham's secretary had apparently been on some errand there, probably in connection with his own visit. He works his staff hard, he thought as he recognised the pale face and severely brushed-back hair-style of the woman Ernest Markham had referred to as his wife and secretary.

Wife? Or 'wife', like Mavis? He didn't know and didn't care. He waved to her quickly, and she waved back as quickly; then she disappeared on the rumbling journey to street level.

Edward Mallow lived in Flat 3 and the door was partly ajar, but Lawrence Brown touched the bell-button to announce his arrival and when there was no response he touched it again, and heard it ring, and when there was still no reply he decided that the M.P. had probably slipped out for some quick word with an occupant of some other flat, would be back soon, and meanwhile had thoughtfully left the front door ajar.

He went into the little close-carpeted hall, noting the narrow marble-topped console-table, the silver salver with three or four unopened letters on it, a brass-bound wooden umbrella-stand holding an umbrella and two walking-sticks made of ebony-coloured wood with ivory handles, and by its side a thoughtful-looking rubber plant in a pot. The soil looked dry, and afterwards he remembered thinking that they don't like sunshine but they need some light and air and water like most living things except bats and mushrooms.

That was what flashed through his mind, and he felt sorry for it because it was going to die, and before very long, too; whereas he himself, of course, was well-watered and aired.

On the carpet by the left-hand wall was something which had apparently been suspended by a looped thong of leather from a nail in the wall. The nail had seemingly come adrift.

Lawrence Brown, tidy by nature, picked it up and laid it on the console-table, recognising it, he thought, as an old-fashioned Irish shillelagh. This one did not seem to have been made of blackthorn but of some other wood, and was of a light-cocoa colour at the top. Otherwise it was the usual bludgeon-type weapon with rough wooden knobs and spikes.

In the dim light of the hall he paid no attention to the exact colour. Blood congeals in a comparatively few seconds, and anyway he was thinking of a foreword for his book, not about congealed blood.

A door on the right of the narrow hall was open, and a light shone from the room. He thought it might be the living-room or study but it was a bedroom, close-carpeted with a blue, thick-pile carpet. The double-bed was covered with a chintz material with a pink rose design to link with the pink walls. Across the end was laid a silk dressing-gown, the material having a Chinese pattern, and a pair of blue silk pyjamas, and at the foot of the bed was a pair of black bedroom slippers with E.M. embroidered on each toe-cap. On the walls he caught sight of two modern oil paintings, pleasant enough as colour designs, representing nothing at all.

The dressing-table with its glass top to protect the wood had a chintz skirt of the same material as the bed cover. On it lay two silver-backed hair brushes, a clothes brush, an ivory hand-mirror and a small silver box.

In front of the dressing-table was a white sheepskin rug and a dressing-table stool painted white with a chintz frill round it.

On the right, on the dressing-table, was a silver-framed studio photograph of a naval rating, and across the left-hand bottom corner the scrawled words 'To Eddie with love from Jimmy.' On the opposite side of the dressing-table was a similar frame containing an enlarged snap-

73

shot of a young R.A.F. aircraftsman inscribed 'To Eddie from your loving Bird.'

Father Brown tiptoed quickly out of the room, frowning thoughtfully. He hadn't realised that it went as deep as that. It seemed too good to be true.

Next door to the bedroom was a small, narrow, characterless dining-room, then a kitchen, and then what must be the general living-room.

The door was half open and he could see the end of a leather-covered settee and beyond that, near a window, a paper-strewn desk, with a coffee-cup and saucer at one side of it, and the back of a high-backed chair, and tucked under the chair he could see the heels of a pair of shining black shoes, and he went into the room without knocking, and said cheerfully,

'Evening, Mr Mallow, it's nice of you to see me at this time of night, I hope I am not disturbing you,' and he went up to the chair, and stopped, and knew that he shouldn't disturb the man in any circumstances, and indeed couldn't disturb him in the usual sense of the word, and that he mustn't touch anything, and certainly not a murder victim. Not that it would do any good to disturb him, but he wanted perhaps to cover with a handkerchief the glazed eyes and gaping wounds in the left side of the forehead.

He knew he mustn't, and he didn't, and backed away feeling shocked to the point of nausea, and sat down on the arm of a leather-covered armchair, elbows on knees, head in hands, until he had recovered a little.

As a priest he had seen Mr Mallow a few times but this was not Mr Mallow, this was Robert Richardson, Mr Mallow's private and confidential secretary, whom Lawrence Brown had also seen, but not often.

The sound of voices and of the flat door closing jerked him from a silent menacing world to the mundane world where people moved, and came and went, and talked, and did not lie sprawled in a chair with a head battered in where there was only a cloying stillness, and he went as steadily as he could into the passage leading to the front door and saw two men wearing grey raincoats hesitating by the closed door, and he said quickly, shakily,

'I wouldn't go in there, something awful's happened, I wouldn't go in.' He pointed at the living-room. 'There's been a – it's pretty ghastly – don't go in, you can't do anything.' He was conscious that he was babbling almost incoherently. 'They wouldn't want you to go in and touch things, the police that is, I was just going to telephone, to telephone the police, and I heard you close the door, it was open like that when I came, and so I went in, but don't you go in. There's a phone in there and I'll go in, but don't you, it's horrible, I was going to phone the police when you came, and I'll go and do it.'

'You don't need to,' the taller of the two men said.

'Yes, I do,' said Lawrence Brown quickly. 'You don't understand.'

'We *are* police officers, sir, you don't need to telephone. A lady in the flat below telephoned. We were returning to the station, sir, after another inquiry, sergeant and me. We phoned to say we were on our way back. Station said the lady had phoned. I said we'd drop in on the way back. I am Inspector Barker, sir, Sergeant Green, sir.' He dipped his hand into a side pocket, flashed an identification card, waved it towards the sergeant. 'What's the trouble, sir? Lady said she heard shouting and struggling noises.'

Lawrence Brown licked his lips and said,

'Mr Richardson, Mr Mallow's secretary, somebody's killed him.'

The inspector and sergeant pushed past him and went into the living-room, and walked round the high-backed chair at the desk and looked at the mess and the cause of it. The inspector said,

'Crude. Very crude. Battered. Death seemingly caused by a blunt instrument, that's what we'd say when I was young, sarge. Blunt instrument.'

The inspector seemed to be in his mid-fifties, stoutly built with grizzled grey hair, good features, but lined, probably with overwork. One of the old type, thought Lawrence Brown, solid, kindly and reassuring. He was glad of it. He was glad the inspector wasn't one of the trendy, stream-lined, factory-built models he'd heard about. Doubtless they were needed in modern conditions but at the moment he was glad the man was an old model.

'Sit down, sir,' said the old model. 'You look shaken. Not surprising. Crude job, very messy.'

Lawrence Brown sat down, on the edge of a hard-backed chair, partly supporting himself with his hands on each side of his thighs.

'Your fingerprints on anything here, sir? Touched anything?'

Lawrence Brown shook his head. 'I was careful not to.'

The inspector nodded approvingly.

'People forget not to touch things. Understandable, but it doesn't help, sir.'

He was moving slowly round the chair again and round the remains of Robert Richardson, hands in raincoat pockets, trilby-type hat still on his head even though he was in a house, and a house with death in the living-room. Peering at the floor round the chair, down the sides of the chair, at the top of the untidy desk, under the desk, under the chair. After a while he said to the sergeant,

'Phone Charlie at the station. Tell him to lay things on, surgeon, photographer, fingerprints, two uniformed cops, the usual form. Nothing to the Press yet.'

The sergeant nodded but he said, 'Not this phone, there's one in the street opposite.' He pointed towards a white telephone on the desk and the short length of severed flex coiled round the base. He went downstairs.

The inspector had moved to the high-backed chair again and was looking thoughtfully at what was slumped in it. After a while he said,

'It has been part of my duty to accompany Mr Mallow on certain occasions in view of these troubled times, sir. This is not Mr Mallow. This is – was – a Mr Richardson, as you said, a friend who sometimes stayed with Mr Mallow, sir, and acted as a secretary, as you said. Mr Mallow has been addressing a meeting of constituents this evening. I have just left him. He expressed a desire to stay on and imbibe some beer in a local tavern as evidence of his democratic approach to life, sir. This will be a nasty shock for the gentleman.'

The inspector had removed his hat at last to reveal a round, bald head fringed with dark-brown hair. He sat on a small chair by the window and pulled a notebook out of his raincoat pocket. He said mildly,

'Just a few preliminary details, sir, if you don't mind, seeing you were the first on the scene, so to speak. Your name and address, sir?'

'Lawrence Brown, 312 Palace Road, East Clapham.'

'Occupation?'

Lawrence Brown hesitated.

'Author, I suppose.'

'Suppose, sir?'

'Author. I used to be a Catholic priest, but I left the Church.'

He was not looking at the inspector and felt rather than saw him raise his tired eyes from his notebook.

'I remember the matter – there was a certain amount of publicity in the Press, sir.'

77

'There was. Now I am writing a book about it. For the Catholic and General publishers. And they are going to offer me a permanent job as a sort of religious adviser. Reading manuscripts, that sort of thing. I need the money.'

'Who offered you the job, sir?'

'Mr Markham, managing director. I saw him this afternoon. That's why I am here. I knew Mr Mallow – in the old days, so to speak. I was to ask him if he would write a foreword to the book – if he approved it, of course. He's a Catholic, but a kind of liberal one. This is a dreadful—'

The inspector interrupted him.

'If I may say so, sir, I wouldn't rely too much on getting the permanent job. Not at all I wouldn't.'

Lawrence Brown blinked and felt his heart-beats quicken, and suddenly realised again how much he was depending on a regular salary.

'But he promised,' he muttered, 'only this afternoon he talked to me. And yesterday he said, "We'll see you're all right, boy", that's what he said, he speaks like that, "see you all right, boy".'

'What time was that, sir? Today's talk, I mean.'

'Between three and four. Why?'

'I wouldn't depend too much on the job, sir, like I said things can go wrong. From what I'm told, things have indeed gone wrong, you could say that.'

'Meaning what? He can't have changed his mind so soon, and anyway, how do you know?'

The inspector looked round as the sergeant came into the room and then looked back at Lawrence Brown.

'There's been a bit of trouble, that's what I mean, sir. Mr Ernest Markham isn't with the firm any more. He isn't with anybody any more. We don't know the cause of death yet, sir. But there's mention of stab wounds and head wounds.'

The inspector cleared his throat.

'I take it your talk with Mr Markham was of a friendly nature, sir?'

Lawrence Brown spoke loudly, to drown the roaring, thudding noise of his own heart-beats,

'Perfectly friendly, what are you suggesting?'

'Nothing, sir. I haven't suggested anything, have I, sergeant?'

The sergeant with his long side-whiskers and hard eyes shook his head.

'Nothing, sir, you've suggested nothing.'

'You don't want to say I suggested things when I didn't, sir. That won't get you nowhere. I don't like people who tread on my corns. I get touchy.'

His tone was no longer avuncular and mellow.

The sergeant repeated the words, 'You don't want to tread on his corns, sir. He gets touchy, the inspector does.'

'My apologies, I—'

'Accepted,' the inspector said quickly and indifferently. 'Read that bit you got from the woman, sarge,' he added.

The sergeant flipped open his notebook and began to read in a sing-song tone, 'My name is Rachael Adams— do-da di-da of di-da and I was secretary to the late Mr Markham. I have been employed by him—'

'Skip all that, come to the end bit.'

'Yes, sir. At about three-thirty this afternoon I showed Mr Lawrence Brown into Mr Markham's room. Mr Markham was seated at his desk but rose to greet Mr Brown. They shook hands. Mr Markham was in good spirits and good health. I returned to my room, next door to Mr Markham's, and closed the door behind me and continued my secretarial duties. I could hear the murmur of their voices but could not hear what they were saying at first.

'Later it seemed to me that they raised their voices, as if in argument, and I was able to hear parts of sentences.

79

At about four o'clock I heard what sounded like the voice of Mr Brown. He appeared to be protesting angrily at something. I could not hear the sentence but I heard what appeared to be Mr Markham's voice saying, "Well, that's the way it is." I then had occasion to leave my room for a few minutes and go downstairs.

'On my return I heard no sound of voices at all and assumed Mr Brown had gone. I had not passed him on the stairs but knew that Mr Markham's visitors, when leaving, sometimes used a back staircase with access to his room via a second door. It has more direct access to the street since it obviates walking along the passage.

'Mr Markham usually buzzes for me when a visitor has left in order to dictate a note of any discussion. In view of what appeared to have been a violent dispute I was a little surprised that he did not do so on this occasion, but did not give it much thought.

'At five-thirty I cleared my desk and went into Mr Markham's room to say I was leaving for the day. I found him lying on the floor by the side of his desk. There was a great deal of blood and he appeared to be dead. I telephoned the police. That's all, sir.'

He snapped shut his notebook.

Lawrence Brown had been standing near a standard lamp when the sergeant began to read and he gripped the upright as the statement continued. It was fiction, lies, a fabrication for which, in his shocked bemused state, he could see not the slightest reason. He felt his face suffuse with red, and said loudly,

'She's mad, a raving nut, if she suggests—'

'I am not aware that the lady suggests anything, sir. You appear prone to see suggestions, sir.'

'Just reported the truth as she recalls it,' said the sergeant quickly. 'It's her duty, sir, as a citizen.'

Lawrence Brown once admitted to Mavis that he had a

quick temper. About once every four or five years something could occur which threatened him with a paroxysm of almost uncontrollable proportions. When this happened he was inclined to beat his right thigh, above the knee, with his right hand, though he did not know why; it was an automatic action, and had little good effect. He couldn't talk coherently. His body trembled, and he would try to talk, but few words came out. It soon passed. He had assured her that all she had to do was to wait and say nothing. He thought of her now as he leaned forward, banging his right thigh with his hand. After a few seconds he swallowed and said in a voice hardly above a whisper,

'You don't kill the man you believe will offer you a job – you don't kill him.'

'No, sir,' said the inspector softly, 'no, personally I wouldn't kill him, though I admit there have been times in my career, in the early days, when—'

'And this!' Lawrence Brown's voice was firmer, the emotional tidal-wave receding. He waved his arm vaguely round the room. 'This ghastly business, this looks like a frame-up, that's what it looks like, a frame-up, but why? You don't kill somebody who might help you.'

'Can you tell me of anybody who might wish to frame you, sir?'

Lawrence Brown shook his head. Then, as if to lighten the atmosphere and indicate that his emotions were on an even keel again, he gave a faint smile and said, 'Only the Pope of Rome, and I doubt if he'd bother.'

A sudden thought occurred to him.

'Where's the weapon, the thing that killed him? There's nothing on me that could cause wounds like that.'

Behind him, the sergeant coughed to attract attention. He said,

'While going to telephone, sir, I happened to notice something in the hall on the table, sir. I took occasion to

81

label it, sir, in view of your remarks about a blunt instrument, and have laid it on the hall table once more to await forensic examination.'

The inspector heaved himself out of his chair and went to the living-room door and looked briefly into the hall. The sergeant said,

'It would appear to be a cudgel, sir, made, I believe, of blackthorn, with a knobbly, spiky head of the same wood. It is a somewhat dangerous, old-fashioned, offensive weapon, capable of causing wounds such as those from which this gentleman died, sir. It is known among the Irish as a shillelagh; my wife's grandfather, who was Irish, possessed one, and it has come into my wife's possession. It is, of course—'

He seemed anxious to exhibit his knowledge about shillelaghs, but the inspector shook his head disinterestedly.

'O.K., O.K., but as far as this gentleman here is concerned you won't find his prints on it. So any they find on it—'

Lawrence Brown had been standing in the middle of the room when the inspector went to the door, remembering what he had done when he arrived. For a few seconds he stood quietly, hearing his heart beating rapidly, hearing in advance the lame tone of his voice when he would speak, and knowing he must speak, and that it was now or never.

'As a matter of fact you *will* find mine on it somewhere.' He paused and took a deep breath and forced himself to go on. 'It was lying on the carpet when I arrived. I thought it had somehow fallen off the wall.'

The sergeant said nothing, the inspector just said, 'And?' They both looked at him woodenly.

'I picked it up and put it on the table, that's all.'

The inspector nodded and cleared his throat.

'You made a particular point, sir, when we arrived, of saying you had touched nothing at all in the flat, and if I remember rightly I congratulated you upon that, saying most people weren't so careful. Am I correct, sergeant?'

Lawrence Brown said urgently, 'I meant in this room, I had forgotten about that thing in the hall, I was very upset, very upset indeed, it didn't seem important.'

The sergeant had reopened his notebook and was scribbling in it. He looked up and said, 'Could you explain, sir? You said you had forgotten about it, and then you said that what you had *forgotten* didn't seem important. So—'

'Skip it,' the inspector said. 'He can explain later.'

The inspector hesitated, standing by the desk, glancing down at an array of pamphlets, documents and newspaper cuttings. The dead man had been writing a letter when he was attacked. A ball-point pen lay on the floor beside the chair, an unfinished letter, spattered with dried blood, was still on the writing-desk. He leaned forward and read the sentences on the front of the sheet of House of Commons writing-paper, and said,

'Are you a man of violent temper, sir?'

'Not particularly.' It was the reply the inspector doubtless expected. Ask a silly question and you get a silly answer.

'Let me put it this way, sir – did you have any sort of argument with Mr Richardson? Like the lady said you did with the unfortunate Mr Markham?'

'How could I since he was dead when I got here?'

Lawrence Brown began to beat his right thigh again with his right hand, feeling the rage rising, feeling his face turn pink. He said nothing till the turmoil had passed. The inspector and sergeant watched him. The inspector said,

'I think you *have* a violent temper, sir.'

83

'Look, Inspector, I am not a psychopath. Understand? I am not, repeat not, a psychopath. I know what you are thinking—'

The inspector looked across at the sergeant, who was now standing by the window, looking out, as if expecting at any moment to see the police murder team arrive – the detective superintendent, who would take over from the inspector, and the little band of experts, the uniformed officers. The inspector said,

'He knows what we are thinking, sergeant.'

The sergeant smiled briefly. 'He must be a clever gentleman, sir,' he murmured and turned his gaze down to the street again. Lawrence Brown shook his head despairingly and put a hand up to his forehead.

'Look,' he said, his voice now steady, 'a man doesn't kill the secretary and friend of somebody if he hopes he will help him with a foreword for his book. Motive, where's the motive?'

The inspector picked up the unfinished letter from the desk, holding it gingerly by one corner.

'This was probably a letter Mr Richardson was writing, sir. You could say they were probably his last words on a certain subject, in more ways than one.' He had pulled a pair of thick horn-rimmed spectacles out of his breast pocket, where they had lain folded without a protective case, and put them on, then adjusted them carefully and read in a flat voice,

My Dear Mr Markham,

In view of our telephone conversation I have again considered your request that I should write a foreword for a book by Mr Lawrence Brown, the former Catholic priest.

Let me say at once that as a friend I wish you well with this publishing venture, not only because of your generous periodic contributions to my election fund and personal expenses.

I do not feel, however, that in view of the proposed contents it is the type of book with which I should be publicly associated.

I have been and still am particularly influenced in this matter by the views of my friend and secretary, Mr Richardson, who is highly experienced in these matters and indeed in all public relations affairs.

As I told you on the phone, I shall be delighted to see Mr Brown this evening, when I will explain to him fully the reasons for my decision, such as the importance of not offending the Catholic voters in a constituency where I only had a marginal victory at the last election. I am afraid that this decision is final, unless Mr Brown can convince me, and in particular my adviser in these matters, that there is reason to change our minds. I am sorry. As I say, I wish—

He replaced the letter carefully on the desk, took off his spectacles, replaced them in his breast pocket, and said,

'The last wish is unfortunately not known. Mr Richardson appears to have been interrupted before he could record it, sir.'

'That's not a motive for killing a man, Inspector!' Lawrence Brown spoke loudly, explosively, and instantly regretted showing a glimpse of his hot temper.

The inspector was looking at him, saying nothing. The sergeant had turned his head and was also looking at him. Again he thought he knew what they were thinking, and again he was wrong.

'That woman, Rachael what's-her-name, was going down in the lift just as I arrived,' he began hopelessly.

The inspector sighed and said, 'No, sir. This is not a

woman's murder. Too messy. Revolvers, yes, poison, yes –
but not this sort of thing.'

'There was a man with her—'

'Can you describe him, sir?' the inspector asked
patiently, almost wearily, as though soothing a tiresome
child.

'Not really. He was standing behind her, see? I got a
glimpse of a grey overcoat and part of a grey hat.'

The inspector nodded. 'Might have been anybody, really
– some other occupant of these flats.'

He couldn't deny it.

'Might have been,' agreed Lawrence Brown reluctantly.

The inspector, who had been staring down at the carpet,
suddenly raised his head and said,

'You don't need to say anything and you don't need to
write anything but if you'd care to give us a written statement, sir, setting out everything you know, as it were, it
would help us.'

'Help us a lot,' confirmed the sergeant from his post by
the window.

Lawrence Brown looked towards the chair in front of
the desk, and what was in it, and said,

'Can we do it somewhere else, Inspector?'

'I was going to suggest that, sir.'

'Kitchen or bedroom?'

'Not here, sir. We'd be in the way, we would.' He looked
at his wristwatch. 'They ought to be here by now. We'll
run you down to the station, have a cup of tea, and then
you can write out what you want, sir. It's best, really, sir.
Nothing to worry about. Just tell the facts, sir, just tell
the truth.'

'I'll tell the truth all right,' Lawrence Brown said
bitterly. 'Don't worry, I'll tell the truth, I don't know
what's behind this but I'll tell what I know.'

'That's all you need do, sir.'

Lawrence Brown looked at his own watch.

'Can I ring my wife?'

'Wife?'

'Well, my common law wife, you could say.'

'That what she's called?'

Lawrence Brown's eyes smouldered.

'We're both modern, Inspector, forward-looking, as it were. We don't hold with superstitious ceremonies.'

'It's your choice, sir.'

'Yes, it's our choice. It'll take some time, writing it all out. She may get worried.'

'Look,' said the inspector gently, 'you don't need to ring her, sir. We'll run you back home before we go to the station and you can explain things, right?'

'Well, that's kind of you. Women worry.'

'So do men, sir. And you can pick up a suit of clothes at the same time, sir, and a shirt, and a razor and tooth-brush.' He cleared his throat and said awkwardly, 'We'll need to borrow the suit and shirt you're wearing, sir. Have it forensically looked at. Just a formality, of course, seeing that you had nothing to do with these crimes. Shall we go?'

He looked towards the sergeant. 'You'd better stay till the others arrive. Then you can knock off, right?'

He moved out of the living-room, his arm linked in Lawrence Brown's in comradely fashion, into the narrow passage, past the shillelagh on the side-table and through the front door.

'We'll walk down, as it's only three floors, sir,' he said, and Lawrence Brown nodded.

The car was outside, dark-blue or black, clean and gleaming in the light of the street lamps. It was an anonymous car in the sense that there was no blue light on the roof to emit beams and warn private motorists who had drunk too much to turn down handy side-streets.

A driver was sitting smoking at the wheel when they came out and hastily threw away the remains of his cigarette.

Lawrence Brown sat in the back seat with the inspector, and when they had crossed the Thames and reached Clapham he guided the driver to Palace Road.

Neither the driver nor the inspector spoke and he himself spent the time wondering how to break the news to Mavis. Despite his past attempts to be modern and trendy, permissive and understanding, to blame all crime on the social system, he had not in his heart approved of her attitude to Ron Flint and his friends. He hoped and believed that he could wean her away from her criminal contacts. Conscious of his good looks and personality and persuasive tongue he was confident that it was only a matter of patience and time.

Now, ironically, he was glad that through Ron Flint she had some knowledge of what she would regard as normal police ways of thinking and acting. Curiously enough he himself felt no resentment against the inspector beside him. Nor against the sergeant. One way and another, he thought, they had acted very civilly indeed, and very tactfully, too. He had to admit that had he been in the inspector's place he would have acted exactly the same.

All his emotions and resentment were concentrated against something he could not define. For want of a better description he called it Fate. Deep down inside him he knew instinctively that he had been framed but there were questions to which he could not find even the beginnings of answers.

Why had Ernest Markham been murdered? And in that connection he felt no resentment against the woman, Rachael Adams, either. She had apparently merely reported what she considered the truth. But why was she in the lift when he arrived?

Why had Richardson been murdered? He accepted the inspector's view that it was not likely to be the crime of a woman.

Why had he, Lawrence Brown, been chosen as the one to be framed?

At one point he was aware that the inspector had broken into his thoughts with a murmured question, which he now asked him to repeat.

'Have you had much worry lately, sir?'

He thought for a few seconds before answering.

'A certain amount, I suppose. In my position it is always difficult to ensure a steady livelihood. It is worrying when others are dependent on you.'

'And you are dependent on others, such as Mr Markham and even to some extent, perhaps....'

The inspector delicately forbore to complete the sentence. He produced a packet of cigarettes and offered them.

'No, thank you. Mavis smokes herself but doesn't like me doing so. She fusses about my health.'

After a short while the inspector coughed and said casually,

'In certain cases where extreme worry or harassment can be proved, affecting the health, it is sometimes possible to introduce a defence of diminished responsibility, sir. It is just a thought, sir.'

But he wasn't falling for that one.

'I have done nothing to which I need plead diminished responsibility,' he said primly as they drew up outside his basement flat. 'And I look to the future with complete confidence.' The car stopped.

'You *do* that, sir, you *do* that thing. It makes it easier,' said the driver, pulling back the handbrake. It was the first time he had spoken during the journey.

Lawrence Brown opened the passenger door and climbed

out. The night had now become very cloudy and dark and cold and he suddenly felt nervous and lonely and fearful of the look in Mavis's eyes when he told her about things. Ron Flint's burglaries were one thing but to be suspected of two murders was rather different.

From the interior of the car the inspector called a question.

'Will you be long, sir?'

He shrugged and replied, 'Perhaps ten minutes or so.'

'We'll wait here, sir.'

He thought that was also decent of them. But then he recalled that he hadn't been charged with anything and was theoretically accompanying them of his own free will.

'You can relax, there's no back door,' he said pointedly, and went down the area steps to the one and only door. The curtains had been drawn but light showed through them.

He let himself into the basement kitchen and made his way towards the living-room, calling her name once and then again more loudly, and when there was no reply he looked at the clock on the chimney-piece and saw that it was twenty minutes past ten, and he frowned. He didn't mind her going round the corner to the pub for a quick one in the early evening. He knew she got lonely. But she must have gone out for one before closing time, and lingered on, and he didn't like her being out late. Then he saw that the living-room door was not shut and the light was on in there, and he called her name a third time.

A radio was switched off and he felt a sense of relief as the door opened, and then a return of disquiet, and then utter bewilderment and alarm, as a woman who was not Mavis came out of the kitchen and said,

'They phoned to say you were on your way here. I thought you might like a cup of strong tea. I've put sugar in, do you like sugar? If not....'

He nodded quickly. 'Yes. Thank you. I like sugar. Where's Mavis?'

He was staring at her as he spoke, and took the cup of tea from her, and still stared at her as he sat down in a chair on one side of the grate. He had only seen her three times, on the two occasions when she had ushered him into Ernest Markham's office, and once, briefly, that evening as she came down in the lift from Edward Mallow's flat; but there was no mistaking the severely drawn-back hair, the big grey eyes, or the rich, musical voice.

'Where's Mavis?' he said again more loudly. 'Where is she?'

He thought he knew but he wanted to have that point, at least, cleared up.

'I thought she would be here, waiting for you.' Her cool grey eyes looked at him reflectively. 'Drink up your tea, Mr Brown. You are shivering.'

'I've had a shock, a terrible shock,' he said and took another gulp of the hot, strong tea. Somehow the whereabouts of Mavis did not seem so important now. 'In fact two shocks. Mr Ernest Markham—'

'He promised you employment. And he was a man of his word.'

'That's the point, isn't it? I mean, he *was* a man of his word but he isn't now, is he? He's not a man of anything, he's not a man at all, is he?'

'There's something I have to explain.'

'There's quite a lot you have to explain,' he murmured and took out his handkerchief from his breast pocket to wipe away the little beads of perspiration forming on his forehead. 'I don't feel very well,' he said quickly.

'What sort of not well?' she asked quietly.

'Bit sick. And muzzy. Sick and muzzy.'

'You could do with some fresh air, I expect.'

He heard the door open behind him and guessed it was Mavis at last, and realised with a feeling of vague surprise that he didn't really care where she had been, that in fact in the last few minutes he had forgotten all about her and her whereabouts.

But he struggled to his feet to greet her, and as the inspector and the driver came into the room alone, without Mavis, he heard the woman, Rachael Adams, say,

'Mr Brown is not feeling well. I think he needs a little fresh air.'

Lawrence Brown steadied himself, placing one hand on the back of the chair in which he had been sitting. He said querulously,

'She's not here. You brought me to see her and collect some clothes but she's not here.'

The inspector shrugged and said, 'I'm sorry.'

'I'm sorry, too,' said Rachael Adams, and laughed. 'It is better to take one bite at a cherry than two.'

He was perspiring more freely and talk of cherries and bites at them meant nothing. He began to tick off certain items with the forefinger of one hand and the fingers of the other, saying, 'Suit. Shirt. Underpants. Socks. Tie. Shoes. Suitcase in cupboard....'

He swayed and nearly fell and the inspector caught him and said,

'The air on the way to the police station will make you feel better.'

They assisted him out of the basement flat and up the area steps and into the big dark-blue saloon car. He sank back against the upholstery in the rear passenger seat. The inspector went round and got in by the off-side rear door and sat beside him on his right. The thin driver, surprisingly, squeezed in and sat on his left. Between them he could hardly move.

In point of fact he didn't mind. He didn't want to move. The sickness had worn off now but the drowsiness had increased and he closed his eyes because the effort to keep them open was almost painful.

Nevertheless, he forced them partly open when the driver's door opened and shut and the thin sergeant who had done the driving before was still at his side. After peering through half-opened lids he said in a slurred voice,

'Why's that woman driving? Why's Rachael Adams driving?'

'The old sergeant had a few nips of whisky while we were waiting,' the inspector said soothingly. 'It wouldn't do for him to have to breathalyse himself, would it?'

He closed his eyes again, but muttered, 'Why that woman?'

'She helps us now and again. Rachael will explain later.'

'When you've had a good night's sleep,' Rachael Adams said in her deep, musical voice.

'Or two good nights,' the sergeant suddenly said, and laughed.

'Maybe three,' the inspector said softly. 'Two full days and three nights, then you'll be rested.'

'Properly rested indeed,' agreed the sergeant. Rachael Adams accelerated, then slowed down to turn left into Clapham High Street.

On the corner, a middle-aged man airing his brown dog watched them. It would have been difficult for Lawrence Brown, even if he had been awake, to know for certain whether the man had raised an arm to adjust his hat or to give a discreet greeting. But the strong sweet tea, or rather what was in it, had now taken full effect and he neither saw the man nor heard Rachael Adams say,

'Everything go well?'

'Dead easy.'

'No trouble, struggles, telephone calls, scenes to attract attention?'

'Went like clockwork,' sniggered the man who was a sergeant. 'Pity we've missed the girl.'

Since the woman and one of the men was not speaking any tongue known to Lawrence Brown it didn't much matter whether he heard the remarks or not.

CHAPTER 7

Although Vandoran's migraine headache was over he was still what he called 'listening'. He envisaged migraine as a sort of animal hiding in the undergrowth, head on paws, waiting to spring out when the victim least expected it.

Sometimes, when the main attack was long over, the animal would make a second, almost playful, little rush at him. He had been told that this was rare and that therefore he was an interesting case. This annoyed him because the one thing he never wanted to be was an interesting case of any kind.

So now, two days after the disappearance of Lawrence Brown, he sat at his desk overlooking Regent's Park 'listening' for any rustle in the undergrowth, and when Reginald Sugden came into his room Sugden recognised from the look on his face exactly what he was thinking. In his down-to-earth Yorkshire way Sugden took the view that either you succeeded or you failed, either you had a migraine or you hadn't, and although Vandoran was by no means a hypochondriac there were occasions when Sugden felt no sympathy for him.

Vandoran was looking at some newspaper cuttings on his desk, pulling them towards him with his right hand and trying to flatten down the unruly quiff of hair on the crown of his head with the other hand. He pushed three cuttings across to Sugden. One was a single-column story:

PUBLISHER KILLED IN
HIS OWN
OFFICE

A secretary clearing up for the night found the dead body of her employer at his desk.

He appeared to have been stabbed several times after being hit on the head.

The dead man was fifty-year-old Mr Ernest Markham, head of the Catholic & General Publishing Company. He was unmarried.

His secretary, good looking, dark-haired Miss Rachael Adams whose family lives abroad, said,

'As far as I know Mr Markham had no personal enemies. He took over this business when it was in serious difficulties and has built it up to its present success. I do not know what will happen now.'

Scotland Yard believe that Father Lawrence Brown, the Roman Catholic priest who gave up his vocation in the Church for love, may be able to assist them in their inquiries. Last night Father Brown was not available. It is known that Father Brown has negotiated a contract with Mr Markham's firm.

Sugden tossed the cutting back across the desk and said, 'Aye, well, that's as may be. From what I've heard, Father Brown is not the only author who'd like to thump his publisher.'

'Thumping's one thing, killing's another.'

'Some authors wouldn't be too fussy either way.'

Sugden had picked up the other cutting. The main headline was across three columns this time:

MP'S AGENT MURDERED IN
LUXURY LONDON FLAT

The body of Mr Robert Richardson, publicity agent and political public relations officer privately employed by Mr Edward Mallow, Tory Member of Parliament for East Clapham, was last night found battered to death in Mr

Mallow's flat in Eaton Terrace, off Sloan Square, London.

The discovery was made by Mr Mallow when he returned from addressing a meeting of his constituents and he immediately summoned the police. Mr Mallow said last night,

'I do not know who would wish to murder poor Bob Richardson. He lived on the premises in order to deal with the innumerable inquiries with which an M.P. may have to deal at any time of the day or night. He was about thirty years of age, a most likeable fellow, and had worked for me for some three or four years. I think he hoped to stand for Parliament himself one day.

'I suppose it is possible that robbery was the motive. But nothing seems to be missing except two framed pictures of friends of mine which I kept on my dressing-table. They were valueless, I would think. It is tragic and puzzling.

'I have only recently moved in here from Clapham because it is more handy when the House is sitting,' Mr Mallow continued. 'This is the second most distressing event for me within a few weeks. I am a Roman Catholic and my former parish priest, Father Lawrence Brown, developed personal problems not so long ago, and left the parish, and indeed the Church. It was a great blow. It is not for us to be judges of our fellow-men in such matters, and indeed I had invited him to have coffee and brandy with me last night. I had hopes that it still might be possible for him to arrange his life differently. But I was back rather later than arranged and I did not see him. No doubt he thought he had misunderstood the day.'

'He's a bit accident-prone,' Sugden said and handed the cuttings back.

Behind him he heard a light, formal knock and the door opened, and Vandoran's secretary came in with an early edition of an evening newspaper and laid it on his desk and pointed to a column on the front page. Vandoran read it and handed it to Sugden, saying nothing, merely pointing at the column as his secretary had done.

THE PUZZLE OF
A MISSING
PRIEST

Anxiety is felt for ex-Father Lawrence Brown, whom the police think can assist them in their investigations into the deaths of Mr Ernest Markham, the publisher, and Mr Robert Richardson, friend and public relations officer of Mr E. Mallow, M.P.

At her home in Palace Road, Clapham, Mrs Brown said this morning,

'I expected Larry back three nights ago. The last I saw of him was when he left in the afternoon for an appointment with Mr Markham, who was going to publish the book he is writing.

'In the evening he left a note here to say Mr Markham had asked him to call on Mr Mallow that evening, and in fact had made an appointment for him to do so because it was important. Mr Markham wanted Larry to persuade Mr Mallow to write something for the book and Mr Mallow had said he was reluctant to do so.

'Larry said he might not be back till around midnight. I went out and had a few drinks with some friends and there was a bit of a party and I got back very late. Larry likes me to keep up with old friends.

'But he did not come home and has not telephoned. He was expecting big things of Mr Markham, I know, and his death must be a great worry to him. He knew Mr Mallow, too, and the awful thing that happened in that house must have upset him. I do not know if he knew Mr Richardson. He probably did. I am very worried in case these shocks and worry have caused a loss of memory.'

A watch is being kept at all air and sea ports but Mrs Brown informed Scotland Yard that her husband had taken no clothes with him and had not withdrawn any large amount from the bank. Apart from possible loss of memory she fears he may have had an accident despite the fact that she has received no reports from a hospital or police station.

'I must just go on hoping,' she said.

Sugden pushed the newspaper back across the desk.

'You want to get a hair-cut,' Vandoran said suddenly by way of friendly comment. 'You look awful.'

Sugden nodded. 'Aye, I do want to get a hair-cut and I do look awful.' He ran a hand over the fuzz growing down the sides of his face and felt the back of his neck where the bristly black hair was beginning to fall over his white shirt collar.

'What I want to do and what I ought to do are different. I'm growing it for the bloody Service. At great personal sacrifice, an' all.'

Although he had not lived up north for many years, when annoyed he still reverted to his flat Yorkshire accent. 'I'm not getting it cut, 'cos a short-back-and-sides sticks out like a sore thumb, it does. You go into a pub with a short-back-and-sides and people stop rabbiting and stare at you. Bad for trade.'

He tapped a thin sheaf of papers on his lap.

'What's it in bloody aid of?' he asked peevishly. 'Is this one of your Fun Games, because if so—'

Vandoran shook his head.

Sometimes, when he concealed himself by the pond's edge and looked at the scene, he indulged in what he called a Fun Game. This he likened to a fly-fisherman casting a fly into an eddy of water or a stretch of water dappled by sunlight passing through the branches of a tree. There was often no reason why a fish should be there but experience and intuition told him there was no real reason why a fish should not be there. Sometimes there was, usually there wasn't, and Vandoran's Fun

Games were not appreciated by his staff, who had enough to do without indulging in investigations based on nothing.

Vandoran's thin lips parted and the wide, frog-like mouth began slowly to stretch across his face and the almond-coloured eyes listened. He knew his boys referred to his sporadic investigations as Fun Games and thought it was a good description, even though, now and again, some of the Fun Games didn't turn out to be such fun after all.

He shook his head again and said,

'Not a Fun Game, not from where I'm sitting.'

'Tell.'

Vandoran had a system which was unpopular in the Registry where they kept the files. Every name which came prominently to notice in the Press was looked up, just in case Registry could turn up something of interest.

'There is only one trace,' Vandoran said now, picking up a piece of paper and reading from it. 'Markham, Ernest, query real name: Ruben Markovitch. Born 1925. Member of British-Ukrainian Friendship Society 1965. Resigned 1966.'

Sugden looked blank.

'You suggesting the Russians—'

'Not suggesting anything yet – just exploring. Now you tell. You know more than I do – I hope,' he added.

'I saw this priest, Brown's side-kick at the presbytery, Father Davidson, youngish, quite friendly, willing to help. Before he bunked off with this floozie, Father Brown did the usual parish duties. Masses, marriages, funerals, confessions, raising funds, visiting the sick, bazaars, all that sort of lark.

'Now what you asked for – rich and influential Roman Catholics in the parish,' muttered Sugden and shuffled the sheets of paper on his lap.

'Including lapsed Catholics,' murmured Vandoran. 'Including lapsed Catholics, particularly lapsed Catholics.'

Sugden nodded. He said drearily, 'It's a longish list.'

'Narrow it down.'

'To what?'

'What I asked for – List Three. That's the important list.'

Sugden ignored him. He said,

'They overlap, you know. Lists One and Two. List One, Practising Catholics, and List Two, Lapsed Catholics, they overlap. There should really be a List One "A" – Really Practising ones, and List One "B" – Nominally Practising ones.'

'Funny word, "practising", what do they practise at, on whom does a practising doctor practise, his patients?'

Sugden ignored him again and said patiently,

'Take the local Tory Member of Parliament, Ed or Ted Mallow, he's an overlapper. He's sure of the Tory voters. Fairly sure, anyway, even if he goes to Mass. But he wants the Catholic vote, see, and they could be dicy if they think he's lapsed. So he goes to Mass. Not often, but now and then. But he doesn't go to confession or Communion. He's lapsed really, that's what this bird Father Davidson said.'

Vandoran raised his eyebrows. 'I thought priests didn't talk about the confessional. Seal of the confessional and all that.'

Sugden shook his head.

'You got it wrong, you got it all wrong, you have. It's not *who* goes in that's secret. It's what's *said* that's covered by the seal of the confessional. Stands to reason, doesn't it? Nothing secret about who goes in. You can sit on a bench outside the box and watch who goes in, can't you?'

'If you say so.'

'I do say so, I've been into this in a big way, see? A priest can say old Bloggins turned up at confession tonight – first time for six months. He's a rum one, he is, he can say. He can say that, especially to his side-kick in the presbytery, and it's O.K. But he can't say what old Bloggins told him in the confessional, he can't say exactly why old Bloggins is a rum 'un, he can't, no, he can't. Nor even hint at it, he can't. See?'

'List Three,' Vandoran said laconically.

Sugden sorted out a sheet of paper. He read the heading aloud,

' "Rich or influential lapsed Catholics who have been very seriously ill in the last twelve months." '

He stopped and sighed. His heart wasn't in it. Vandoran could see that. Sugden said,

'It's short but it took the priest bloke some time to think it out. He had to scratch his head, the priest bloke, see? Lapsed or nearly lapsed, or overlappers not being in close touch, see? Names: Davis, Smith, Edwards, Flint and Mallow, the M.P.'

'Go on.'

'Chap called J. Davis, local councillor, builder. Could have swung the housing committee to put contracts his way. Nothing to be proved, of course. Had a coronary seven months ago. Recovered. Woman called Felicity Smith, buyer in a big store. Rumour said she bought substandard goods at full price and got her cut from the supplier. Just rumour, like I said. Thought she had advanced womb-cancer. Had an operation. She hadn't. F. Edwards. Known to have spent time in prison. Housebreaker. Another coronary. Bad one. Everyone thought he'd had it. He had. He recovered a bit, then snuffed it. R. Flint. Professional gangster, mugged a night-watchman once so as to let his gang in. Did time for it. Knifed by a pal, Flint was. Nearly died and didn't, and more's the pity. Then there's Mallow.'

Sugden paused and put his papers down on his lap. Vandoran said,

'Who heard the confessions?'

'This Father Davidson heard the woman. Smith and the house-breaker Edwards. Nothing secret about that, except what they actually confessed. They were in hospital.'

'And Father Brown heard the others?'

'I suppose so.'

'You "suppose so"?'

'That's what he said. I asked him. "Father Brown, I suppose," he said.'

Vandoran's mouth began to stretch, as at the beginning of a smile, but his eyes did not lighten and the smile never developed.

'They are all still alive, except Edwards?'

'Well, they were yesterday evening, as far as the locals know.'

Vandoran got up from his desk and walked about his room for a few moments. He had a springy gait; and his big, brown-shod feet made no sound on the thick blue carpet. Eventually he stopped and sat on a corner of his desk facing Sugden.

'This bloke Mallow -- what was his trouble?'

'Pain in his belly, dramatic loss of weight, a lump in or around the liver. He thought the obvious but it wasn't. They took the lump out. A cyst – benign, as they call it in their daft way.'

'You ever been a lapsed Catholic, or a nominal Catholic, or an overlapper, as you call them?'

'No, I haven't that,' replied Sugden in broad Yorkshire tones, 'and I haven't been an Eskimo either, if you want to know.'

'I would think, and I expect a lot of other people would think the same, that if such citizens are taking a long hard look at death something religious may pop up, like a residual tail. There's no harm in taking out a marginal insurance like confessing even if you're lapsed, nominal, or overlapping. It's free, there's no premium.'

He looked at Sugden. He got off the desk and began walking about again.

'What are you thinking?'

'I'm thinking it's still a Fun Game,' said Sugden sourly.

'I bet that monkey Father Brown isn't thinking that. If he is, he shouldn't be. He may have signed his own death warrant with just four words tucked away casually in those bloody pornographic articles in the *Sunday News*. "A self-admitted atheist." You realise that?'

'I don't get it,' Sugden said flatly. 'Not from where I'm sitting,' he added, using Vandoran's favourite current expression. Vandoran had an irritating habit of picking up an expression and wearing it to shreds.

'You're thick as a brush sometimes, Reg.'

'Plank, thick as a plank is better. Daft as a brush.'

'Plank, thick as a plank,' Vandoran repeated obediently. 'Not always, just sometimes.'

'Thanks.'

'I've been keeping these few newspaper cuttings,' Vandoran said.

Sugden laughed and put a match to his thick, stubby pipe.

'Just for fun – Fun Game, as I said?'

'At the beginning,' Vandoran admitted reluctantly. 'Maybe at the beginning – not now. Not a Fun Game now.'

He had some more cuttings on his desk roughly held together with a paper-clip. He didn't hand them to Sugden but glanced over them and said,

'You want to read the popular Press more, Reg.' He picked one out and read it aloud to Sugden.

' "Ex-priest disappears", that's the headline. It says: "Father Brown, the former priest who left the Roman Catholic church a couple of months ago in order to marry one of his parishioners, has disappeared. Even his worried girlfriend, Mavis, does not know his whereabouts.

' " 'I know he was worried and embarrassed by the publictity which surrounded him,' she said yesterday. 'I believe he has gone into seclusion somewhere in order to finish writing a book he was working on about his experiences in the priesthood. I do not know where he is and he has not been in touch with me, but I am not worried. We have a joint bank account.' " '

Sugden passed a hand over his coarse black hair and said,

'Seems possible.'

Vandoran said, 'You think? For a sex-mad, besotted priest to cut himself off from the floozie who caused all the fuss? You think? Anyway, she doesn't stick to her story. One moment she's worried, the next she isn't.'

'I said, "seems *possible*",' muttered Sugden, filling the air with clouds of thick smoke, a form of camouflage he indulged in when not sure of himself. 'Perhaps he was fed up with her – found something better.'

Vandoran looked at Sugden, his brown, almond eyes expressionless, long thin lips compressed into a narrow curved line.

A totally ruthless frog, Sugden thought, not always merciless or unfeeling but cold in planning and carrying out anything, however unpleasant. He watched as Vandoran moved over to a bookcase and flicked over the pages of a reference book and ran a finger down one of the pages. Then he snapped it shut and replaced it and went back to his desk chair.

'I think he's dead,' Vandoran said bleakly.

Sugden took his pipe out of his mouth and stared at Vandoran, wide-eyed and motionless.

'Suicide?'

'Not suicide. You've seen the girl.'

'Briefly, as you said.'

'And the note?' Sugden nodded.

'The note doesn't figure for a suicide. I'd expect "Forgive me", or "Can't live without you", or "My mind is going". Sad little stuff like that. Not just "Cooked myself some eggs and bacon. Off to see an M.P. about the book. Back about midnight. I love you." Not stuff like that. What's she like?'

'Small lush type. Blonde, brown eyes. In her early thirties, curling a little round the edges, as some blondes do, but quite edible. The note was signed Larry. She called him Larry.'

'Did she really?'

Sugden coloured. There were occasions when he almost disliked Vandoran and his sarcasm.

'Yes, she did,' he answered irritably.

'And may one ask who she thought you were?'

'One may,' snapped Sugden. 'She thought I was a London representative of a north-country newspaper group. She is sure the note is genuine. And she is sure he will contact her soon. I hope he does, I quite liked her.'

'I bet you did.'

'Not that way,' Sugden said patiently. 'She's a Newcastle lass, north-country like me, she's got character—'

'Enough character to steal a priest, and turn him atheist, and so have him killed – after he's made his will, I hope.'

Sugden shook his head and said nothing.

'You don't get it, do you,' said Vandoran.

'Nope,' Sugden replied.

'Consider List Three. A local councillor, maybe dishonest, maybe not. A gang leader. A Member of Parliament. The rest don't count.

'Each thought he might be dying and made a last confession to Father Brown. Nobody knows what was said and what wasn't said, nor in what detail. Dying men, or those who think they are, talk freely if they've got the breath. Especially under the seal of the confessional.'

Vandoran paused, then made the point clearer.

'It doesn't matter, you see, because even if they recover they're in no danger, nor is anybody else, until....'

Sugden was looking at him, his head slightly lowered like an Anglo-Saxon bull in a furrow. Vandoran stared back.

'Tick-tock-tick-tock. Anything stirring?' he asked.

'Aye, there is, an' all. You mean this priest type, being now an atheist, doesn't care a damn about the seal of the confessional. He's free to talk if he wants to, if he thinks he ought to, that's what you mean.'

Vandoran nodded. Sugden looked down at the short list of names on List Three. He said,

'Can't see the woman Smith or a town councillor murdering a priest. The house-breaker Edwards has had his chips already. Flint's a small-time gangster.'

Sugden waved his pipe. 'That leaves Mallow, the M.P. Think an M.P. is going to stalk Father Brown and gun him down?'

'Not Mallow,' Vandoran said.

'So?'

'Mallow's friends.'

'What friends?'

Vandoran leaned forward and laid his hands, palms down, on the desk, one on each side of him, fingers outstretched and separated, fan-wise, forearms curved inwards; each hand was also turned inwards at an angle of forty-five degrees; the elbows were bent and he had lowered his head so that his chin was almost invisible below the almond eyes and thin, wide mouth. My God, he looks like a frog, thought Sugden with a mixture of awe and near apprehension, wondering if Vandoran was about to spring forward across the desk at him.

'How do I know what friends?' Vandoran said, and his rasping voice seemed to sound like an angry croak. 'Member of this Parliamentary Sub-Committee and that, including the Forces Estimates Committee, dealing with what money would be allocated to which arm of the Forces, and why, and how it would be spent. A sitting duck for any foreign intelligence service. And maybe this duck quacked. He thought he might be a dying duck in his last thunderstorm. So he quacked, loud and clear, to his priest.'

'Maybe he didn't quack much,' interrupted Sugden loudly.

'Maybe he did, and maybe he didn't, and maybe he did and said he didn't, would you risk it if you were running a valuable agent like that? What would you do? Suppose you were a Russian K.G.B. man. You wouldn't kill the duck, you'd kill the man he'd quacked to. You'd protect the duck – whatever doubts you had – wouldn't you?'

'Probably,' said Sugden at once. 'That ex-priest is possibly so stuffed with dynamite he's like an unexploded bomb. I'd explode him if I were them and if Mallow is what you think.'

'Or defuse him.'

'Explode him. Bang. Gone for good,' Sugden said. 'No good fiddling about in hope and doubt. Dispose of him.'

Vandoran said gently, 'Ducks and bombs, bombs and ducks, it boils down to this – is he, was he, a good insurance risk?'

'Not in Yorkshire he wouldn't be, not for my money.'

Vandoran raised his head from his frog's hands and said,

'Nor for mine. He never had a chance. I think he's dead. Find out,' Vandoran said, a few seconds later.

'That's a police job,' protested Sugden sullenly.

There was no reply. Sugden watched the thin-lipped smile spread across Vandoran's face. Sugden sighed and said,

'It's past my bed-time. I must get back to my desk.'

Vandoran was still smiling his cold frog-smile as Sugden stumped to the door. Then he called him back.

'Go back to the girl, Reg. Have a long, long talk. Get the pattern of their lives. Especially hers, now. You know something? I reckon she's no better an insurance risk than Father What's-it. If the duck quacked to the priest, they'll reckon the priest could quack to his dolly-bird.'

CHAPTER 8

Sugden sat in the Sportsman's Bowl, Clapham, sorting out
his approach method, wondering what he'd say. It's a
burden, thought Sugden, that's what it is, it's a burden to
be told a secret. At first you can feel flattered by the trust
but in the end it's a burden, and it can become a health
risk, a bloody menace, that's what it can become. He felt
almost sorry for Father Brown, as sorry as his blunt,
practical Yorkshire temperament allowed.

The bloke hadn't asked to be told secrets, it was his job,
he'd been sent for. Mallow had sent for him to come to
the nursing-home because Edward Mallow, M. P., thought
he might kick the bucket.

As like as not, the other side knew he might be sick
unto death and, lapsed Catholic or not, guessed he might
send for a priest before what might be the fatal operation.
Last-minute clearing of the soul's conscience, marginal
insurance, like Vandoran had said, costing nothing except
perhaps to the priest bloke. Like as not they'd kept the
nursing-home under surveillance, maybe they had an
agent inside, perhaps indirectly they partly owned the place,
kept it as a sort of sick-bay for agents in dicy health. Anyway, he guessed they knew about Lawrence Brown's visit.

A sudden thought struck him, a logical extension of
speculation. The private room where Mallow had lain in
bed, was it clean or was it bugged? He fondled his pint
of beer, turning it this way and that, holding it up to the
light, thinking that men made a lot of fuss about whether
beer was clear or clouded, and it didn't make a damned
bit of difference to the taste. The landlord was leaning on

the bar watching him. He didn't like customers holding up their beer, it put ideas into people's heads.

He shouted across to Sugden, 'It's all right, innit?'

Sugden drank a third of his pint at a gulp and nodded happily. The landlord was a bald-headed, red-faced, retired sergeant-major type. He saw Sugden smile, and smiled back, relieved.

Sugden wasn't smiling at him. He was smiling at his thoughts, and they weren't about beer. They were about Edward Mallow, M.P., murmuring to his confessor priest, 'And I have sold State secrets to a godless country which persecutes Holy Mother Church.' And Mallow later saying to his spy master, 'I didn't say anything about our work, of course. It wasn't on my conscience. I'm working for peace am I not? That's not a sin.'

And the soothing reply, 'Of course, of course,' even though they had at their office a transcript from the bugged room which showed he was lying. 'Keep him in play,' they would have decided. 'Keep him in play, *at least for the moment*. Later on, well, we'll see.'

There was a sudden burst of laughter from the other end of the saloon bar. Mavis Bailey had come in and was singing a Geordie song. He could just make out her small lush form, in yellow blouse and dark-blue trousers, the long blonde hair, and he caught an occasional glimpse through the male figures surrounding her of her happy, flushed face and sparkling eyes. She was beating time on the counter with her beer-mug, the beer slopping over as she sang 'Cushie Butterfield' though without the Geordie accent.

> 'Her name is Cushie Butterfield and she sells
>   yellow clay,
> And her cousin is a muckman, and they
>   call 'im Tom Grey—'

She waved her free hand, trying to get them to join in the chorus, but they didn't, not knowing the words, not being Geordies.

Sugden picked up his beer-mug and got to his feet and strolled over to the bar counter and stood on the outskirts of the group, watching her sing, watching the others as they, too, watched her, silent but smiling. Suddenly, at the appropriate moment, his strong voice with its northern overtones joined with hers, as he sang:

> 'She's a big lass an' a bonnie lass an' she
>   likes her beer,
> And they call her Cushie Butterfield an' I
>   wish she was here!'

She swung round the moment he joined in, looking at him delightedly, and when the last verse was finished she said loudly,

'Hello, again. Good old you! You a Geordie?'

He shook his head.

'Yorkshire, but I lived in Newcastle for a while. My favourite county, Northumberland is. After Yorkshire, of course. Good beer up there.'

'You don't get it down here,' she said sadly.

'Miss it?'

'I got problems. You can't have everything, can you?'

'You can have a brown ale,' Sugden said and picked up her glass. A voice behind him said,

'It's ordered already, mate.'

He turned. A man with a grey, rubbery face was looking at him. He wasn't smiling. Nor were the others. Sugden said,

'You boys want anything?'

'Bit of privacy, that's all. Not much to ask, mate, bit of privacy, not hurting anybody, not at the moment, just a bit of privacy, mate.'

Sugden shrugged, and picked up his half-empty pint mug.

'Sorry, love,' he said to Mavis Bailey. 'See you sometime.'

'See you,' she said, and looked him in the eyes as she spoke. But the fun had gone out of her face.

He strolled to the far end of the bar, hearing footsteps behind him as he moved. He put his mug down on the counter, and hoisted himself on to a bar stool. He felt rather than saw somebody join him on his left side. Rubber Face said,

'Don't, mate.'

Sugden turned his solid square head and half turned his equally solid square body.

'Don't what?'

'See her, like you said.'

Sugden tried to convey surprise with his eyes.

'It's a sort of way of saying goodbye,' he said.

'Keep it that way. My name's Flint,' he added, apparently thinking it would mean something.

Sugden shrugged indifferently.

'O.K., O.K. Why? Her husband back?'

Flint looked at him suspiciously.

'You a cop?'

'Newspaperman.'

'She's had enough of them. Get me?'

'Is he back – the priest bloke?'

'Not yet.'

'Heard anything from him?'

'Not yet.'

Sugden nodded, seemingly satisfied.

'O.K., then. That's all I wanted to know, see?'

'O.K., then. No harm done,' Rubber Face said.

'No skin off your nose,' agreed Sugden.

'None off yours, mate, neither, not yet. Me and my pals

are keeping an eye on her, see? Especially me.'

He turned to move away.

'See you,' said Sugden. Flint paused for a moment before walking away.

'Best not, mate. Best not for you, that is. Don't want no trouble on this patch, mate.'

He nodded and rejoined his group. Ramsden the landlord sidled up to the bar counter.

'Drop of Scotch to go with the beer,' said Sugden. Ramsden turned and put some into a small glass and brought it over to Sugden.

'Got any ideas for tomorrow?' he said loudly.

'Horses or dogs or birds?' Sugden asked, equally loudly.

'Horses.'

'Don't bet on 'em. Big bookmaker told me, "Got it worked out," he said, "you bet regularly with me," he said, "and you'll win sixty per cent of your cash back, meaning you'll lose forty per cent, suits me," he said.'

'Mug's game,' agreed Ramsden, pulling himself a glass of bitter.

'Have that one on me,' Sugden said. 'Nobody else will.'

'Thanks, guv. Cheers. Mug's game,' he repeated, and wiped his mouth with the back of his hand, 'but I like it. Bit of fun, worth the money, well, almost. That's Ron Flint,' he added in a low voice. 'Done time for being rough, see? Bookie when he's not inside. So he says. Probably bookie when he is. I lose to him regular. He likes it that way,' he added, lips hardly moving. 'Spends good money here.'

'Your money.'

'Probably. He likes it that way.'

'Takes all sorts,' said Sugden meaninglessly. The landlord thoughtfully agreed that it did take all sorts to make a world. Sugden had a mental pigeon-hole full of phrases like, 'Takes all sorts,' 'It never rains but it pours,' 'Two's company, three's none,' 'Here today, gone tomorrow,' few of them true, but they were handy. He called them Sugden's Stoppers because they plugged what might be conversational gaps.

Looking across the room he saw Mavis Bailey glance at her watch, say something to the group and go out of the pub.

'She come often?'

'Most evenings, for an hour or so. Likes a bit of company. Doesn't spend much herself.'

'Gets treated, like tonight?'

'That's it.'

'Husband come with her?'

'Not often. People stare at him. He looks after the baby – when he's here. He's done a bunk. A few days ago. Police are looking for him.'

'Why?'

Ramsden replied, hardly moving his lips,

'Murder, double murder. The baby's up north with her mother. She's on the loose, and when I say loose, I mean it, guv.'

'*His* baby?'

'No reason to suppose it isn't,' muttered the landlord carefully, and began swabbing down the bar counter with a dirty cloth.

'What do *you* think?'

'I don't think, guv. Doesn't pay to think, not round here it doesn't. If you've gotter think you want to think about your health, guv.'

'First things first,' agreed Sugden, producing one of his Stoppers.

He waited until Mavis Bailey had been gone a quarter of an hour. Then he nodded to the landlord and strolled out, crossed the High Street and walked along to where it joined Wilkes Road. The street where she lived was the second turning on the left, one of several streets of tall, early-Edwardian houses, begrimed with smoke, divided into layers of flats and bed-sitting rooms; doomed to destruction in the near future, to be replaced by concrete blocks of what councils called 'dwelling units'.

Meanwhile they lingered on, architectural slag-heaps in which human termites currently burrowed and made their little temporary homes while they looked apprehensively at the future, wondering where they might eventually build a small, secure nest. Here, in their fear-laden existence, the stricken termites shared their insecurity with each other; speculating about their futures, doing each other's shopping in cases of illness, sometimes visiting each other in the evening to play a game of cards and drink coffee ('Not too strong, dear, it keeps me awake'), and to grumble about the landlord who wouldn't spend money on a slag-heap which was doomed.

Eventually, no doubt, they would find a nest, perhaps in a council flat in a high-rise block, and there would be some sort of below-floor central heating, and hot water, and electric lifts which sometimes would be wrecked by vandals and sometimes be inoperative because of power cuts. And nothing to grumble about except old age and complete silence.

Letter to the council, thought Sugden, letter to the council: 'Dear Sir, When I shut the door of my flat there's complete silence and something ought to be done about it, and nobody tramping up and down stairs, and something ought to be done about it. There's a young couple opposite on my landing, and they play radio and television all the time, and they don't want to know if I'm well or ill, alive or dead, and something ought to be done about it. It's the silence, see. The Welfare said they'd get me a cat to talk to, but it's not allowed by the council. Where I come from was a dump and so's this, but different, it's the silence, they ought to do something about it. Yours faithfully,' and which was worse, thought Sugden, a physical dump or a spiritual dump, and they ought to do something about it, but what he didn't know, and nor did anybody else, he knew that, too.

No malice, everybody trying to do their best and not knowing what was the best. I'd settle for the old dumps, he thought as he walked along but he knew he wouldn't be allowed to. And even here there were some things you couldn't do, some people you couldn't visit, even if you wanted to and they wanted you to, and if you couldn't keep a cat or dog in a high-rise block of flats neither could you visit Mavis Bailey in a very low-rise basement flat, not without permission from rubber-faced Ron Flint, so-called bookie and obviously boss of local mobsters.

But he was going to visit her all the same, because he had some more questions to ask her. He was beginning to agree with Vandoran. The disappearance of the ex-priest wasn't a Fun Game. What it was he didn't yet know but it wasn't a Fun Game of Vandoran's. He inclined to the view that pure crime or a personal quarrel was involved; in which case it was a law-and-order problem, a police problem, not involving Vandoran or his department. But he wouldn't have bet on it with any bookie and certainly not with Ron Flint.

He heard footsteps close behind him but he didn't look round. The street opposite her basement flat was deserted except for a shabbily-dressed middle-aged man showing the gutter to his brown mongrel dog on the other side of the road.

Sugden walked straight past her flat to where he had parked his car further up the road. He started the engine and turned left at the first cross-roads, and parked on the left about a hundred yards up the street, and some four or five minutes' walk from Mavis Bailey's basement flat, and smoked his pipe. As he had driven past her flat he had seen through the driving-mirror that the man and his dog were going up the front steps of a house nearly opposite Mavis Bailey's.

CHAPTER 9

She pulled him inside and hastily closed the basement door when she saw who it was. She said,

'Sticking your neck out a bit, aren't you? Mine, too, come to that. What's the idea?'

'Larry,' said Sugden curtly. 'I want to talk about him – not for publication. I promise.' She looked at him gravely.

They were standing in the living-room. She hesitated, shrugged, and said, 'Want a beer?' What she'd seen she liked.

'Please.'

She went to a cupboard, took out two tins and tore them open, and handed one tin to him with a glass and motioned him to sit in an easy chair. She sat herself on the settee and balanced her glass of beer on the arm.

'If you want to know why he's freaked out, I can't tell you for sure.'

'Some say he's afraid of the police.'

'He's not the type to run out on that sort of trouble.'

'Others think he's suffering from loss of memory.'

She crossed one trousered leg over the other, nearly upset the beer-glass, caught it in time and said,

'I don't think so.'

Sugden said nothing. He thought if he asked her what she really thought she would run for cover. She had to come to it gradually. Ten seconds is quite a long time for a silence to last. In the end she said,

'I think he is scared. Plain bloody scared, but not of the police. That's why he's done a bunk.'

'Of Ron Flint?'

She shook her head.

'Ron never threatened him. Ron knows me. Ron was prepared to wait. He's clever that way, is Ron. Course if some outside bloke tries to horn in, like you did tonight, well, that's different. Otherwise no. Ron's prepared to wait, like he is now.'

'Love—' began Sugden. She interrupted.

'I don't love anybody for long periods.'

'Larry?'

She frowned slowly, considering the matter in her level-headed north-country way.

'I thought it might be different. Larry was vain, o' course, vain as a peacock, he was, but that meant he kept himself clean, took trouble with his clothes, elegant he was, and knew it, had real education, too, used to gabble poems at me and say things in foreign languages, and he wasn't bad at making love once he got the know-how; not like Ron, but not too bad, one way and another.'

'Which way and what other?'

She looked at him and smirked. 'I thought it might all be different. Him being clever. But it wasn't different. Meaning I wasn't different,' she added in her honest way. There was a short silence. Sugden flung in a Sugden Stopper,

'Leopard doesn't change its spots.'

'This leopard doesn't.'

Sugden began to beat up slowly to his target.

'Going to miss him?' he asked gently.

'You want the plain truth?'

'It helps sometimes.'

'The answer's no,' she said thoughtfully. 'I was getting fed up, he was dreamy, romantic some would say. It's all right for a bit, like eating Turkish Delight stuff. Sickly after a while. Ron's a proper bastard in some ways, but colourful, see? Always on the go, never a dull moment. Broadminded, too, that's why I'll go back to him – for a bit – that's why he'll have me.'

Sugden nodded. He could fire now. The target was unimpeded. The last thing he wanted at the present, or any other time, was a hysterical woman, but he saw there was no danger of that, the ground was clear.

'You said you thought he did a bunk because he was scared.'

'Yes. Bloody scared. And I don't think he'll come back.'

'You don't? How would *you* know?'

'I don't know. I said I don't *think* so.'

She stirred impatiently and flung her cigarette-end untidily into the hearth. It lay smouldering acridly near the grate.

'Stop pussy-footing,' she said irritably. 'Come clean. Tell what's on your mind.'

Sugden took a deep breath and fired.

'I don't think you'll see him again.'

'I said so myself, didn't I? More or less. So what?'

'I think he's dead,' said Sugden flatly.

She swallowed the sip of beer she had taken and put the glass carefully on the carpet beside her and looked at him, frowning from troubled eyes.

'I wouldn't like that, really I wouldn't. He was a nice guy in many ways, I wouldn't like to think he'd been knocked off, not Larry.'

'Who said anything about him being knocked off?' asked Sugden quickly.

'I'd hear if he was sick, or if he'd been in an accident. Larry knocked off, I wouldn't want that. There's one or two of Ron's pals I wouldn't shed tears about, nor that ape opposite with the brown dog, come to that, but old Larry....'

She stopped and he saw her lips were trembling. He

thought of a Stopper, like 'Here today, gone tomorrow,' but knew it wouldn't do, and instead paraphrased a couple of lines from Pudney's poem and said, 'Better by far for Larry the bright star to keep your head and see his child is fed.'

'It isn't his child. He was easy to kid. It'll be fed,' she muttered.

Now he had to do the follow-through, now he had to press her. If he didn't he could see Vandoran's wide smile. He might not say much, but his cynical smile would say a lot, like, 'O.K., don't explain. She was a lush doll looking sad for the moment, so you didn't press her.' Almost without knowing it he translated his own thoughts, 'You're a lush doll, looking sad for the moment, feeling sad – just for the moment.'

She glared at him indignantly.

'I'd shop him, if somebody's killed Larry I'd shop whoever killed him, if I knew, which I don't.'

'How long has he been scared?'

'Since we were together. Even in Portugal when we were, you know, pretty turned-on, he'd go on the balcony sometimes and look down and say, "Who's that man down there?" or sometimes "Who's that woman looking up here?". I'd say, "Who the hell do you think it is? Think the Pope's agents are gunning for you?" but he didn't even smile, and once on a picnic, by a stream, when he was spouting something about a loaf of bread and wine, he suddenly stopped and looked along the stream up to a little bridge and said, "What's that car doing there?" Gave me the creeps a bit, at first, but after a while I took no notice, "It's psychological," I told myself.'

'Psychological?'

'Him maybe having a guilty conscience, in a way, whatever he said. That's when I went off him a bit, really, it wasn't the soppy romantic stuff, like I said. A girl doesn't like living with a bloke who seems to be seeing spooks everywhere, does she? 'Cos it went on here in London, see. When telly shut down he'd sometimes say, "I feel like a breath of fresh air, coming?" So we'd take a trot round the block, and sometimes he'd say, "Who's that?" and I'd say, "It's that old geezer with his dog," and he'd say, "It's got a bad bladder, that dog, always in the street," or he'd see somebody standing in a doorway, or going round the end of the street here and stop and look thoughtful.

'Gave me the creeps,' Mavis Bailey said again, 'it wasn't natural. I gave him a piece of my mind now and again, but it didn't make no difference – well, it did for a bit, and then he'd be back at his old game again, and that's why I think he was scared. A girl can't live all her life with a type who's scared of spooks everywhere. Well, I mean, can she? So I wasn't going to be sorry to see the last of him, no, I wasn't, but now you've gone and said. . . .'

Her voice trailed away and she licked her lips. Sugden got out of his chair. He said,

'Spooks don't kill, love. And they don't make people vanish without trace, either, dead or alive.'

She finished her beer and went to the cupboard and tore open another can of it and refilled their glasses, saying, 'Muck. Gnat's – well, gnat's water,' she said in a pseudo-refined voice, 'not like the Newcastle stuff.'

'There's always a reason—'

'Not for this stuff,' she interrupted, pointing at the beer.

He took no notice. 'There's always a reason if you dig deep enough.'

'Well, dig, Buster, dig away,' she said softly, and got up and poured some whisky into two small glasses as chasers with the beer, and tossed hers back and handed a little glass to Sugden. He got out of his chair and took the glass.

'Backbone for the beer, Buster. Put some lead in your pencil.'

'Not needed. Ron wouldn't approve.'

The drink had given her courage. She laughed and said, 'Ron can go and—' She left the sentence unfinished.

She did not finish the sentence because he kissed her, telling himself that it was in the line of duty, that he wanted to learn more about the spooks, that it was a good idea to soften her up, though he did not think Vandoran would accept the argument.

She was good at kissing, she liked it. He could tell that by the way she caressed the back of his neck and pressed herself to him. He wasn't surprised Ron Flint liked keeping an eye on her. He'd come out of prison at just the right time. She was lonely and worried, ready to renew the old game. He wondered what would happen when the ex-priest returned, if he ever did.

He began to steer her gently towards the settee in front of the electric fire, not with any particular idea of cementing a new and beautiful friendship in a practical way but simply because he was tired of kissing her standing up.

He had his right arm round her shoulder. He said, 'You're strong but your bones are as slender and light as a seagull's.'

'Skinny, eh? I've been called some things in my time but—'

The crash and tinkle of falling glass in the next room interrupted her. He pushed her aside and ran into the kitchen next door and saw the jagged hole in the window, the mess of broken glass and something oblong shaped, wrapped in paper, lying on the floor. He switched off the light at once, turned and nearly collided with Mavis in the doorway.

'Maybe you got some friend who's lost his front-door

key,' he said tartly. 'Maybe it's just a cry for help, as some psychologists say when a thug beats up an old lady. Maybe I can help him,' he muttered and made for the front door. She called after him,

'Let it be, love! It's probably Ron, let it be, they'll only do you, they'll go over you, love, let it be!'

But he took no notice. As he opened the door he called back to her, 'Go in the other room. Don't touch the thing on the floor in the kitchen. Don't touch it!'

He ran out of the front door and up the area steps to the pavement. The street was nearly deserted. Most of the denizens were indoors eating their evening meal, or cooking it over a gas ring, and in the halls of the houses would be a smell of frying onions. But on the opposite side of the road he saw a youth with tallow hair standing with his bird.

He ran across to them and said,

'See anything, see anybody throw anything in that house I came from?'

'Nah. Didn't see nothing.' He spoke defiantly.

'Nothing? No car? Not two or three men – or one man – running?'

'Nah. Nothin', like I said.'

He began to pull his girl along as he slowly moved away. To Sugden she was just a short figure and a white blob of a face, dimly seen in the bad street lighting.

She called back to him over her shoulder as they slouched off,

'We didn't see nothing, see?'

He nodded. In this district it was healthier to be like the three wise monkeys, see no evil, hear no evil, speak no evil, in fact not speak at all if you could help it. Further along the man with the brown mongrel dog was again going up the steps of his house. Sugden ran along the pavement and up the steps after him as the door was closing. He put his foot against it and pushed it open against resistance.

In the dim hall lighting the man glared at him. So did the dog, smooth-haired body sloping forward as it strained against the chain attached to its collar. Its head was spade-shaped, broad in the forehead, narrowing to a pointed but strong muzzle, and the eyes were the same chocolate colour as its muscular body.

Its owner was of medium build, aged perhaps fifty or so, and wore a shabby, belted brown overcoat the same colour as the dog and a mottled grey cloth-cap.

On either side of the cap was grey hair, still showing some faded yellow, and his straggly grey moustache was nicotine-stained. The face was bony, of indeterminate shape, like the nose which had a small wart on one side of it; the complexion and nose were the colour of the heavily-addicted beer-drinker, and the small blue eyes were hostile.

He jerked at the dog's chain and said, 'Sit dahn, you! He don't like strangers. You want sumppen? There's a bleedin' bell, yer know.'

He turned his hot, angry eyes to Sugden and said again, 'You want sumppen?'

'Somebody threw something into the basement opposite,' Sugden said hopelessly, knowing he would get nowhere. 'See anybody?'

'Heard a crash, put me coat on, and the lead on the old dog to take 'im out – takes time. Nobody in the street except a young chap and his girl.'

'Saw you out with the dog not long ago. Your dog incontinent or something?' Sugden asked.

'Likes a breath of fresh air, the old dog. Goes to the pub with me. Old dog always has a drop of my beer, 'e does.'

The blue eyes were beginning to blaze. Sugden said,

'Now you're back. Short visit? Or didn't you get there?'

'Forgot my pipe, see?' Suddenly the impertinence of the questioning struck him. 'What's the matter with yer, snooping around, you a cop or sumppen?'

'Newspaperman.'

'Can't believe a word you read in the papers.'

He turned and stumped upstairs, dragging with him the brown mongrel dog. His rubber-soled shoes made little noise on the stairs, less in fact than the clicking of the dog's toe-nails on the old-fashioned linoleum.

Before he disappeared round a bend in the staircase he stopped and shouted down, 'You want to mind your own business, that's what you blokes ought to do. World'd be a better place.'

Then he had gone. Sugden wondered where the man and dog had been hiding immediately after the crash and sound of broken glass. Perhaps in some basement area, watching him till his back was turned as he talked with the long-haired youth and his bird, then nipping quietly along to his own house, not wishing to risk some house-owner coming out and seeing him skulking there?

Abruptly, from somewhere in the street, without sound of quarrelling, came the sound of a woman screaming, then the words, 'No, don't!' Then, just as abruptly, all was quiet again.

Sugden let himself out and ran across the road and knocked loudly at the door of Mavis Bailey's basement flat. She opened it at once.

'You all right?' he asked.

'Course I am.'

'I heard screams.'

She shrugged. 'It's like that round here. You get used to it. Larry used to rush around at first. I told him to lay off. He got used to it.'

She was wearing thick leather winter gloves and was

holding a brush and dustpan. Some of the large pieces of glass were stacked against a wall.

'I'll pin a blanket over the hole,' she said.

'Go in the other room, love, while I see what this thing is.' She shook her head. 'It must be heavy to smash the window like that. It's not a bomb, it's a bleedin' brick.' He thought she was probably right but one lived in strange times.

It was wrapped in white paper and the paper was held in place by three thick elastic bands. Sugden took out his pocket-knife and knelt down. He did not cut the elastic bands but made a cautious small incision in the white wrapping-paper. Through the slit he could see what indeed appeared to be the rough surface of a brick. He gently picked it up and felt round the sides. It was of one piece and nothing was attached.

He nodded and looked up to see Mavis Bailey watching him, brown eyes alert and interested.

'Sentimental present from Ron Flint? Why didn't he come bursting in if some pal saw me come here and told him?'

She sighed and said,

'He's got a one-track mind, he has. Maybe he was going up to the White City, dog-racing. Maybe he got word around for somebody else to chuck it. He's got friends.'

'Like a man with a brown dog?'

For a moment she looked puzzled.

'"Old dog always has a drop o' my beer",' quoted Sugden.

'Oh, him! Holding his glass of brown ale down and letting the dog lap off the top – disgusting I call it. Silly old fool, Ron never talks much to him.'

Sugden had removed the outer wrapping. Inside, tied round the brick, was a sheet of quarto-size paper, also white, with some words written in black ink with a broad felt pen, encased in an ink-drawn square.

> TO HELL WITH THE POPE!
> DOWN WITH THE SCARLET
> WOMAN OF ROME!
> PRIESTS OUT! OUT, OUT, OUT!

Sugden smiled sourly. 'He's out of date, he's no longer in touch, he obviously doesn't believe your Larry left the Church. He said he doesn't believe a word he reads in the papers.'

'What's on the back?'

He turned the sheet of paper over. This time the words were typewritten, but unevenly, clearly by an amateur. He read them and handed the sheet to Mavis. She read:

TO THE SLAVE OF THE ROMAN APOSTOLIC DELEGATE OF SATAN! YOUR ROMISH PLOTTING DOES NOT DECEIVE ME! OUR GREAT QUEEN ELIZABETH WHO SENT TO TYBURN GALLOWS THE DEVILISH BETRAYERS OF CHRIST'S CHURCH IS GUIDING ME! I DROVE YOU OUT OF YOUR CHURCH, NOW YOU PRETEND TO HAVE LEFT VOLUNTARILY. NOW YOU ARE IN HIDING, BUT YOU CANNOT HIDE FROM ME, PRIEST FROM HELL. YOU PLOT DOWN THERE IN YOUR SECRET PRIEST'S HOLE, SCHEMING TO BRING BACK THE INQUISITION, THE FIRE AND THE STAKE. YOU CARRY OUT YOUR BLASPHEMOUS MASSES, I HAVE SEEN THE WHITE CLOTH AND CANDLES ON THE IDOLATROUS ALTAR YOU CALL A TABLE. FLY, ROMISH PRIEST, FLY BACK TO ROME, YOU AND ALL LIKE YOU, BEFORE THE VENGEANCE OF THE LORD STRIKES YOU! I HAVE THIS DAY SENT DETAILS OF YOUR PLOTTING TO THE HOME SECRETARY.

CHAPTER 10

Mavis Bailey handed the paper back. She said, 'He threw an egg and a bad tomato at Larry during his last mass. I suppose he thinks that drove him out. I didn't see him in the shemozzle.'

'What did drive Larry out – sex? Your sex?'

She looked at him, half amused, brown eyes widely open, and thought for a moment.

' 'Spect,' she said, and nodded happily.

Sugden thought, she's a consort of crooks, perhaps an abettor of crooks, she's sexually disloyal and will probably ditch almost anybody, but she's got a broad streak of unhypocritical, childish honesty. He said casually,

'Know where he lives, this nut?'

'You daft or something? 'Course I do – if it's him. Opposite, he lives opposite. "Old dog always has a drop o' my beer",' she quoted.

Sugden thought of a pair of blazing blue eyes, fanatical, a little mad, perhaps, and told her how he had seen the man three times in the street with his brown dog, appearing from nowhere the last time, apparently thinking he could make it from a basement-area hiding-place back to his house without being seen.

'Go over and pat his dog or something, next time you see him in the pub. He knows you're the "Romish priest's woman", as he'd call it. See how his eyes blaze as he looks at you, hating you. Try it.'

She looked at him silently for a few seconds, trying to work things out.

Then she led the way into the living-room again, away

130

from the street, and went to the cupboard and brought out another two cans of beer and began pouring it into two glasses. He sat in an armchair. The time for kissing was past.

'You and Ron Flint going steady then?'

'I never go steady. Except for a while, so long as it suits me. Ron knows that. When he was inside I went for Larry. Quite fun, really, having a go with a priest.'

'Aye, I bet it was an' all,' Sugden muttered, inadvertently dropping back into his native Yorkshire.

'Now Larry's not here, there's Ron. Worked out quite well, really.'

'What happens when Larry comes back?'

She handed him his glass of beer.

'He won't come back,' she answered calmly. 'He's freaked out.'

'He's *what*?'

'Freaked out, like I said before. Gone. And for good,' she added. She saw the puzzled expression on his face. 'Up north we'd say booggered off, not knowing much about modern culture in the south.'

'*Wee-ee* yer boogger,' Sugden said, in the vernacular, in a hard voice indicating total disapproval and surprise. 'Why? What made him do it?'

She took a long slug at her beer, saying nothing. Sugden put a light to the tobacco in his pipe, and said,

'He left a note saying he'd be in touch, and some money I suppose?'

'No money. But we had a joint account. Keep me quiet for a bit, till the cash runs out, give him a head start.'

'No row with you? No warning? Nothing?'

'Nothing. On the Thursday he said he was going to see his publisher to collect some money as an advance on his book, and he didn't come back, except to cook himself a snack. He left a note saying he was off to see an M.P. or something, and the publisher's secretary, she can't help. "Perhaps he's gone off to the country somewhere to write his book," she said. "Without any clothes," I said, "you want your head examined."'

She lit a cigarette and sat down on the settee and balanced her glass of beer on the arm, and said,

'Perhaps he got fed up with me. Wouldn't blame him, once he'd had enough of you-know-what, 'cos he's brainy and I'm not. Perhaps he got fed up with the baby, washing the baby's clothes, he always did that, I'll say that for him, or fed up with living in this basement, and not being, well, you know, a somebody, a priest is a somebody in a way, isn't he? Perhaps he missed that.'

Sugden nodded, but she saw he wasn't really listening and asked,

'What's on your mind, hinny?'

'Want to talk about something.'

'Nothing to stop you. What?'

'Confessions,' said Sugden abruptly. 'Did Larry talk to you about the confessional?'

'Now and then,' she said suspiciously, 'but he never said what he heard.'

Sugden had got up and was wandering round the living-room, glass in hand, pausing here and there to look at a cheap framed print on a wall, even pausing to look at the bare wall if there wasn't a print on it.

'Never mind what they confessed. Who were they? Mention any names?'

She swung round and glared at him.

'You're a cop, you said you weren't. You are.'

'Not a cop.'

'Newspaperman, like you said?'

'Not a newspaperman.'

'Liar?'

'Sometimes. If necessary.'

'Well, that's straight. What's your work, you a private eye, private dick, or something? Work alone?'

'Not alone. Got pals,' he said carefully.

'Got a mob behind you?'

'Sort of. Yes – you could say that, sort of.'

'Going to get them to rough up the geezer with the dog?'

'He's just screwy.'

'He can still throw bricks. Do it for me? Rough him up for me?'

'Might – sometime. Depends, doesn't it, depends on what's in it for me, doesn't it?'

'Ron wouldn't like it. He's dangerous, too.'

Sugden shook his head impatiently. 'Not that, not *that*.'

She flared up. 'So I'm not good enough for you? No one would have thought so, the way you were kissing me, hinny.'

'I could go for you all right, hinny,' he said. 'Aye, I could, and make no bloody mistake, hinny. But you're Ron's bird.'

'Nobody's,' she said defiantly.

'Ron's,' insisted Sugden. 'Even if Larry comes back you'll be Ron's bird, exclusive, for a bit.'

'He's colourful, like I said, and he ain't scared, he ain't scared of anybody, and he ain't scared of nobody – spooks is nobody, he ain't scared of nobody. And so—'

'Maybe spooks aren't nobody,' broke in Sugden.

She looked at him in total bewilderment.

'Of course Larry's spooks were nobody,' she muttered.

Sugden nodded. 'Have it your own way.'

'I always do.'

'Don't reckon on it, hinny, don't reckon on it,' he murmured. The mild warning tone of his voice made her uneasy. She remained staring into his eyes for a full five seconds.

133

'Come clean. Tell,' she said at length.

'When I get what I want, and it's not what you thought.'

'What do you want, then?'

'Little talk, that's all, little talk about Larry and confessions.'

'I've told you, haven't I, he never told me what he heard, nothing, and he won't, I know.'

'But do *they* know he will tell nothing, to you – or to the police – or to anybody else? I accept he told you nothing, but do *they*?'

'Who's *they*?' she interrupted.

'Spooks – just spooks. Larry said he saw them. Maybe he did, maybe he didn't.'

'*What* spooks?' she asked nervously.

Sugden shook his head impatiently.

'How do I know? I wouldn't be here if I knew, would I? Now he's an atheist, do *they* know he'll keep his trap shut? What about this book he's supposed to be writing? He won't name people. He didn't in his articles, but he'll go into more detail, maybe there'll be hints and traces to be picked up which will mean something to those interested – putting two and two together, pointing to people. There'll be some big secrets, real dynamite, in his head. Think he's a good insurance risk?'

When she made no reply he said again,

'Think he's a good insurance risk?'

She still remained silent, worried.

'Or *was* a good insurance risk,' he added relentlessly. 'Maybe that's what I should say, think he *was* a good insurance risk?'

'I hope he's not dead,' she whispered. 'I hope he's not dead, he was a nice guy, really, bit soppy, but nice to me. I had fun.'

He wasn't interested in sentimental memories, he was

134

as tough as an old boot when on a job, if he had to be. He noted her words, 'nice to me', 'I had fun,' and he noted how she related everything to herself, and saw he had to pressurise on those lines. He walked once round the dull little room with its cheap furniture, cheap prints, yellowish walls, then said,

'Think *you're* a good insurance risk?'

'Me?' She was partly puzzled, partly frightened.

'Yes, *you.*' He tapped his forehead with the stem of his pipe. 'If he had a lot of dynamite stored in there, how do they know what isn't also stored in *there?*' he said and gently tapped her head with a forefinger. 'They don't know, do they? Think *you're* a good insurance risk if they want to seal off all possible leakages – forever?'

He watched as she shivered and poured out a tot of whisky for them both.

'What can I do? Put a notice in the papers, saying ex-Father Brown never told me anything he heard in confession?'

'Somebody might believe it – simple adulterers, childish fornicators, honest liars and innocent sneak thieves, that lot might. But the big stuff, the heavy squad – the spooks, they're different.'

'Who's my insurance company?' she asked in a voice hardly above a whisper.

'Me. Only me.'

'What's the premium?' she suddenly shouted and tossed back the remaining whisky in her glass. 'As if I didn't know,' she sneered, 'as if I bloody well didn't know!'

He shook his head. 'You've got it wrong again, love. All I want is – names. Names of people whose confessions he's heard. Nothing secret about that.'

She was holding her head in despair, body swaying from side to side.

135

'He only mentioned three.'

'It's a start.'

'It was in Sesimbra, Portugal, little seaside resort near Lisbon – over the suspension bridge, along a motorway, through some woodland, then down a winding narrow road, with a disused monastery somewhere on the right, and they call it a sleepy little fishing village, and the holiday-makers on the beach are as thick as blackfly on broad beans and—'

'I dare say,' said Sugden shortly. She ceased to be an unofficial tourist guide, and said,

'One day he was sitting on the balcony having breakfast with me, reading an old English newspaper, and he said, "These lapsed Catholics, something sticks, you know. When they think they may be dying they often hedge their bets, do a confession, costs nothing, and if they recover, well, no skin off their noses. Maybe we'll be the same." He laughed and so did I. I remember three of them Larry mentioned.

'Those are names I want,' Sugden said urgently, and watched her. She seemed to be genuinely trying to remember.

'One was some local councillor. Think his name was Davis.'

'Fiddling contracts, I'm not interested. Not worth a killing to cover that up. Yes?'

She looked around apprehensively and said in a half-whisper,

'Ron Flint.'

Sugden thought for a moment, and said again,

'Not interested. Small gangster type.'

'Not so small as all that!'

He smiled to himself at her indignant protest and said placatingly,

'Not so small, but local, see? No protection rackets,

gambling, prostitution, drug rings. And he didn't need to kill Larry to get you, hinny. What's his address?'

'Don't know, he contacts me, see? Don't know his address.'

'Telephone number?'

'Don't know. I leave messages at the pub.'

Ramsden, the landlord, wouldn't know it either, thought Sugden, or if he did he wouldn't tell it, him being health-conscious.

'Don't know where he is now,' she said. 'He moves around, see?'

He believed that, at least.

'The third name?'

'A Member of Parliament, he is. Fairly local.'

He flung a few names at her.

'Baker? Maynard? Panter?'

She shook her head.

'Mallow?'

'That's him! "'Marsh' Mallow," I said to Larry. "Tory," I said. "I bet sex came into the confession," I said. "In the Labour Party it's cash, in the Tory Party it's sex." You take your choice. In the Liberal Party it'll probably be both, them being liberal-minded. 'Nother drop of Scotch?'

'No thanks.'

'He seemed real worried about this Mallow. Mentioned him once in his sleep in Portugal. Must have told Larry something ripe and nasty to shock him like that.'

'Probably sex stuff as you say.'

But he only half believed it. Half of him believed that the spooks Larry had seen were solid and wore jackets, trousers and probably raincoats. It wasn't a Fun Game now, and never had been. She hadn't told him anything fresh. But she had confirmed three of the names given to him by Lawrence Brown's fellow-priest and he was beginning to veer towards Vandoran's other opinion. It wasn't just a police job.

Somebody was protecting Mallow, he thought, and the price, to date, had been three deaths. The reason for the disappearance of Lawrence Brown was apparent. But at that moment he saw no reason for the other two killings.

'I think I'll go back north,' said Mavis Bailey suddenly. 'I'll feel safer in Newcastle among the Geordies. All straightforward up there, no spooks or nothing. You've scared me, you have,' she added reproachfully. 'All this guff about spooks and insurance risks. And Larry being dead, and me the next on the list, so to speak. I live here alone and I'm scared.'

He felt the tension mounting inside him, as it always did when he had to make an ethical decision off the cuff. He knew that she was right: she would be much safer up north, and probably happier, among her down-to-earth Geordies. He temporised as the tension grew inside him, knowing what he must do, yet reluctant to do it.

'What about the kid?'

'If Ron wants me and his kid he can follow me. If not, he can jump in the bleedin' Thames. Larry's dead.'

'You psychic?'

'Yes, I am. And they weren't proper spooks Larry saw. They were something else, don't know what, and I got a funny feeling I ought to get back up north.'

Suddenly the tough old boot in Sugden reasserted itself.

'My insurance company can't help you at all if you go north,' he said flatly, but what he meant was that she, Mavis Bailey, couldn't help him, Reginald Sugden, if she went north. He wanted her where she was but the awful thing was that although he thought she might help him he didn't know how. It could prove a fatal and useless gamble. He wanted to keep her handy, yet he knew he could not protect her, not really, not twenty-four hours a day, week after week, month after month. He might if he knew what to protect her against. But he didn't. Nor did she.

Larry the ex-priest knew. But Larry hadn't told her and Larry was gone now and probably wouldn't be able to tell anybody except the Archangel Gabriel; and that was just why he had had to go, taking with him the secret which had worried him, nagged at his conscience; and Larry would be too busy to communicate now, even if he could; busy arguing about why he should be let through the golden gates in spite of everything; he would be preoccupied with his own affairs, would Larry.

The man with the brown dog and his brick was just an irritant, he wouldn't kill her. He might try and convert her with something almost as tiresome as the eggs, bad tomatoes and bricks; but Sugden didn't think he'd kill her. Ron Flint probably wouldn't; he might beat her up, which she might appreciate, but he was too keen on her to kill her, not now that he was sure of her, rightly or wrongly.

'Marsh' Mallow, the Tory M.P.? Sugden hesitated. M.P.s don't normally kill potential voters themselves, not even to cover up past sexual indiscretions. If they did the voters' list would be shorter. He pulled himself together.

'Have some bars put on your windows, a chain on the door, don't open the door when alone at night, don't go out unaccompanied after dark,' he said in uninspired tones.

'And what'll *you* do, eh?'

She looked at him resentfully.

'Make some arrangements, don't ask what. Here's a couple of telephone numbers to ring if you're worried.'

He scribbled his office and home numbers on a page of his diary, tore it out and handed it to her. She sighed and took it, and he knew he had taken on a dreadful responsibility which he couldn't carry out, not a hundred per cent. Or even fifty per cent. It was problematical if he could protect her twenty-five per cent, day in, day out, but he thought he could. Therefore twenty-five per cent of his conscience was clear and seventy-five per cent was not.

Suddenly, in a flash, he knew why he wanted her in London, and the realisation shocked him for a few seconds. He wondered if he had known it all along and had hitherto refused to admit it to himself.

He was using her as bait.

She was the tethered kid. He hoped that he would be on hand with his rifle when the kid bleated and the tiger sprang.

He hoped so, but he felt an appalling doubt about it.

'I'll be off,' he said and moved to the door. She moved with him. Before he opened the door she stood beside him and put her face up, eyes shining eagerly, fear forgotten, trusting him in a curiously simple way.

'Kiss-kiss,' she said.

'Not-not,' Sugden murmured regretfully, because what he had in mind had to be done with total sincerity, his brain not blurred by the feel of soft lips.

He closed the door behind him and went up the area steps and looked at the shattered basement window and turned left at the top, and then eventually left again, and came to his car and automatically looked underneath for trailing wires, and saw none, and went round to the driver's door and saw the shattered windscreen and, inside, the slashed seat covers and a piece of white paper on the driver's seat, and hardly needed to read the words printed on it in block capitals: KEEP OFF THE PATCH, NEXT TIME IT WILL BE YOU, MATE.

He flicked some of the shattered windscreen off the driver's seat and got in and started the engine without qualms, because this wasn't I.R.A. or Arab trouble. This was crude stuff. When he began to move off the heaviness of the steering proved it.

He had been concentrating on the broken windscreen and slashed seats when he had come to the car, and now the car lumbered back to the side of the road and he got out and saw the flat front tyres. Spooks hadn't done it, yobbos had done it.

He switched off, pocketed the keys and made towards the Underground station a few hundred yards north of him. It was an office car and the office recovery unit could fetch it.

He didn't think he would reach the Underground station without interference. He would have been disappointed if he had done.

He carried no firearm. He was not an 007, licensed to kill. He was (unofficially) licensed to wound or hurt, and then only in self-defence, like any ordinary citizen; and if somebody died later, well, it was too bad. A chap is entitled to defend himself.

There was a twenty-yard pedestrian subway leading to the station, down some steps, through a tunnel and up some steps the other side.

He approached it with eagerness, tramping sturdily along humming to himself 'Ole Man River', his unflappable Yorkshire temperament so certain that he would come across what he did come across that he wasn't even thinking much about it, but was trying to decide whether to ring the recovery unit from the station or wait until he arrived home. He decided that immediately forthcoming events would decide for him and felt happier because he reckoned that forthcoming events would demand that he should concentrate on them rather than on Mavis, and now he did so and noted, as he neared it, that a light shone over the entrance to the subway, and that there was a further light at the other end. In between, in the tunnel, there had certainly been another light and the passage had been illuminated, however dimly, but this had obviously been wrecked either by mindless vandals or by others who weren't so mindless.

At the entrance to the subway a girl was standing, apparently straining to see the time on her wristwatch. Her silhouette seemed faintly familiar. He thought she might speak to him on some pretext but she didn't, and he went into the dark passage.

Behind him the girl coughed three or four times. Somewhere here, he knew it would be somewhere here, and now. It would be now.

He was so certain of it that he took out his cigarette-lighter and held it ready in his right hand, waiting for the muttered request he knew would come, and did come.

It came about five yards inside, from the left.

'Can you give us a light, please?'

'Sure,' said Sugden and wheeled left at once and bore down with his thirteen-stones weight, chest to chest, until he had pinned the speaker against the passage wall. Three or four seconds it took and then he flicked his lighter, recognised the long, tallow hair of the youth with the girl whom he had questioned opposite Mavis's flat, and saw the right arm pinned behind the back against the wall, certainly holding the object with which he would have been slugged.

He let the lighter snap shut and fall to the ground and grabbed the tallow hair, one hand on each side of the youth's face, and felt him struggling to release his right arm and the hand with the weapon.

'Drop it, there's a good lad,' Sugden said unemotionally, and while still holding the greasy hair he lowered his grip and dug his two thumbs into the youth's neck where the carotid arteries were situated, knowing he could, if need be, stop the flow of blood to the brain, render him unconscious, even kill him, and knowing that he had no such intention.

When there was no response he said again, 'Drop it, kiddo,' and pulled the head forward and bumped it back twice against the wall, and ran the edge of his shoe down the front of one of the youth's legs and stamped with his heel on the foot underneath, and heard the cry of pain.

'Drop it or I'll break your foot bones, boy, and then I'll crack your skull.' Again he bumped the head against the wall.

The girl at the entrance heard the yell of anguish and screamed something he couldn't understand, and he saw her running back up the steps. Kicks, she'd come along for kicks and she didn't like the reality, and although the words of an old song had no time to form in his mind the sense of them did, and the sense of them was, 'Small fry, small fry, hanging around the pool room; small fry, small fry, ought to be in the schoolroom.' Hanging around Ron Flint, he guessed, kidding themselves they were rubbing shoulders with the big-time ones, currying favour, hoping to be in the big time themselves one day. Serving a sort of apprenticeship, running errands and doing dirty little jobs like smashing windscreens and slashing car seats and tyres.

He heard a thud and clink and guessed that a bicycle-chain had been dropped. So he wasn't a killer, bicycle-chains don't kill, they lacerate and maim but they don't usually kill. Small fry, small fry, hanging around Ron Flint, who wasn't really big time himself though he thought he was, and even Mavis, his bird, was touchy on the subject.

'I've dropped it.'

The words were wheezed out on the wings of a mixture of air, onions, fish and a trace of garlic but Sugden hardly noticed the smell. He was watching the far end of the

143

subway and he saw what he expected to see, which was a youth like the present one in age and build who had been standing in deep shadow, his back to the subway wall.

Now he had stepped from the wall and was silhouetted against the light at the far entrance and was moving quickly and quietly up towards his companion, guessing that something had gone wrong, guessing that help was needed.

He was the back-up guy stationed to dissuade people, if you could call it that, from entering the subway that end while operations were in progress and to lend a hand if required and generally join in the subsequent fun and games, like putting the boot in when Sugden lay helpless on the ground, or having sport with a flick-knife.

Tallow Hair, now that he had both hands free, was beginning to struggle more, trying to wrench at Sugden's wrists. Sugden released one hand from the hair for a second, clouted him heavily across one side of the face, grabbed the hair and bumped his head again, more heavily, against the wall. This time there was an aggrieved note in the protest. 'Jeeze! It's bin dropped, innit? I told you dinnun I, I told you, it's bin dropped, stop bashin' me!'

It wasn't a fight. Sugden got no excitement or joy of battle out of it, it was one-sided small-fry stuff, fully expected when he had seen the mess in his car and the flat tyres, and he had only gone into the fight with one purpose in mind.

'Tell him to stay where he is,' Sugden said coldly, looking sideways over his shoulder. 'Tell him to stay where he is or I may hurt you badly, kid.'

The voice and words sounded loud in the passage-way.

'O.K., Ernie, stay where yer are till I tell yer!'

But the outline of the back-up youth was still moving. Sugden gripped the tallow hair more closely and said,

'He deaf or something?'

'I said, stay where yer are, Ernie, stay where yer are! Do as yer bleedin' told or I'll thump yer!'

The silhouette did not move any more. Sugden said,

'Tell him to go to Ron Flint. Tell him to tell Ron Flint I'm coming to see him, tonight – now.'

'Tell 'im *what*, mister?'

'Tell him what I said to tell him,' Sugden said patiently.

'O.K. Ernie, 'ere, listen. Nip off to Ron's, tell 'im a gent's coming to see 'im now – he's coming now, see?'

Sugden saw the silhouette hesitate uncertainly, then turn and walk slowly back and up the subway stairs and disappear from view.

Sugden relaxed his grip and stood back a pace; then, bending warily down, he picked up his cigarette-lighter and the short length of bicycle-chain.

'You 'urt me, you did,' said Tallow Hair in an aggrieved tone, and stroked one side of his face and felt the back of his head. 'I'll do yer for this one day, yer know that, don't yer?'

'You and what kid's nanny?' asked Sugden mildly.

'Me and the boys, we'll do yer. What you want to see Ron for?'

'Ron wouldn't like his business discussed with children,' Sugden said reprovingly, 'he wouldn't like it at all, you ought to know that, son. You've got things to learn about keeping healthy, you have an' all.'

'You barmy, mister? Ron'll slice you, Ron will.'

'Maybe.'

'Ron and the boys'll slice you, they will.'

'That's life, I guess.'

A knowing look came into the youth's blue eyes and a slow, almost admiring smile spread across his pale, callow face.

'You're bluffing, mister, you ain't going to see Ron. You

got Ernie sent off to Ron to get Ernie out of the way, you
was scared of two of us, you done a trick on me and
Ernie,' he muttered almost reproachfully. 'Know where
Ron lives?'

Sugden shook his head.

'See! Bluffing, like I said, to get Ernie out of the way.'

'I don't need to know where Ron lives, I'm being taken
to him by you. Let's go.'

'Not by me, mister.'

'By you.'

Sugden began to swing the bicycle-chain lightly.

'I got a bird with me, I got to look after her, I got—'

'You got to take me to Mr Ron Flint. The bird's
flown – home probably, yowling her head off. Get yourself a real woman,' he added paternally, 'get yourself an
iron butterfly of about thirty, little canaries won't do you
any good, son, not your sort.'

He wrapped a length of chain round his wrist, and
sighed, and said,

'Can't leave you here. Against the law, boy, against
the law to leave litter about. We going?'

Tallow Head nodded miserably. 'O.K. – but you got to
tell him you forced me to bring yer along. He doesn't
like guys bursting in on 'im late at night, Ron doesn't,
you gotter tell 'im. Ron'll do me, Ron will.'

'Life's difficult, I guess. You walk ahead, son. Far to
go?'

'Five minutes. Short cut. Along the lane, back of the
'ouses.'

The lane twisted between rows of little, ill-kept back
gardens and was unlit. Here and there a lean-to type of
garden shed created a pool of black shadow. Sugden
walked close behind the youth. At one point he said,

'Hope Ernie won't try anything silly, lad, like trying

146

to jump me. 'Cos then you'd be a mess, see, a proper mess, see?'

Tallow Hair said sourly, 'Nah, Ernie'll do what I said to do, Ernie's new, Ernie is.'

The lane ended at a small side-road which in turn led to the High Street. A quarter of a mile away the tall chimneys of a power station reared up against the night sky, then were blotted out as Tallow Hair turned into the back yard of a public house, then into a small enclosed area stacked waist-high with crates of empty beer-bottles.

Small Fry Mark 2 was standing by the back door waiting for them. He said nothing as he opened the door and led the way into a narrow passage.

What looked like a small, forty-watts, naked electric bulb revealed walls which had once been painted a dark dingy green. The paint was scratched and peeling in places. Three or four cheap, framed, coloured prints of old-time prize-fighters hung on the walls, the men stripped to the waist, naked fists raised. Once they had been in the public bar, now they had been crowded out by prints of thin-legged old-time race horses; relegated to the back passage, near the stinking Gents Lavatory.

At the far end of the passage Sugden could see the dimmed lighting of a bar, the landlord listlessly trying to cope with the crowded empty glasses on the bar counter. He was in his shirt-sleeves and hitched his braces up as he turned suspiciously to see who was coming in, and Sugden recognised the bullet head and red face of Ramsden, the sergeant-major type landlord, and knew he was in the Sportsman's Bowl again.

Ramsden came to the bar entrance and looked at Sugden disapprovingly, and said,

'You again, eh? Don't want no trouble, guv.'

'Tell that to Ron Flint.' But the landlord had already swung back to his endless colonies of glasses.

Ernie, the youth, knocked timidly at a door in the passage and a voice from the other side of the door snarled something unintelligible and Ernie opened the door and stood aside to let Sugden go in.

He stepped inside the room. Neither of the Small Fry came in with him and the door closed behind him as the reek of cheap cigar-smoke entered his nostrils, and he saw a haze of smoke curling round the bulb of a standard lamp with a pink shade.

The standard lamp was the only lighting in the room and the lamp stood by the side of a round table covered with a red cloth fringed with old-fashioned bobbles and tassels. On the table, in the middle, was a pack of blue-backed playing cards. Cards had been dealt for four players, two to each, and still lay face down on the cloth, and there were four glasses and four pint beer-bottles.

That was all he made out at first, until his eyes grew accustomed to the light and the shadows; that and the indistinct white blobs of four faces of men seated round the table.

Ron Flint sat by one side of the lamp-standard. Stocky, with grey, rubbery square-cut face, wearing a blue shirt and jazzy tie; his cuffs were rolled back, and dark hair curled on the forearms and some on the backs of his hands; two gold rings were on the third finger of his left hand, one with a small diamond; another gold ring gleamed on the third finger of his right hand. She said he was colourful. Mavis had said that, and Mavis was right.

He looked at Sugden, expressionless, and took a suck from the wet end of his cigar and said,

'You been invited, mate? You been invited to join the card school?'

And when Sugden shook his head, he added,

'You don't take things in, do you, mate?' He tapped

148

his forehead. 'Told you once before this evening, 'aven't I – all I want is a bit of privacy, mate, not much to ask is it? Bit of privacy and peace and quiet, not much to ask, mate.'

'Want to talk to you.'

'You often make social calls at this time, mate?'

'Want to talk to you,' Sugden repeated doggedly.

'What's your name?'

'Charlie Chaplin. What's it to you?'

Ron Flint picked up his glass and took a mouthful of beer. Sugden could see a signal of danger, an angry twitch on the left of the rubbery face – once, then after a couple of seconds another one, and remembered he had more than once risked losing a campaign to win a small skirmish.

'Sugden, Reg Sugden. You can call me Reg,' he said mildly, and his tone seemed to placate Ron Flint.

'You got a mob?'

Sugden thought of Vandoran and his sophisticated organisation.

'Sort of,' he replied without smiling. 'Yes, I got a mob.'

'What you want to talk about?'

'Business.'

Ron Flint leant back in his chair and looked round the table.

'Go on, then – these are my business partners, as you might say. Make it quick, see? 'Cos we want to get on with the cards.'

'Private business,' Sugden said stolidly.

There was dead silence in the room. Ron Flint hesitated, sighed, looked round the table and inclined his head towards the door. There was a rustling and scraping-back of chairs as the other three left the table and went out, the last one closing the door.

Flint sat down, listening, then got up and went to the door and opened it and said, ''Op it,' and came back muttering, 'Cheeky bastard, can't get no privacy round here,' and sat down again and turned his grey face to Sugden.

'Want a beer, mate?' he said unexpectedly, in almost a friendly voice, and reached down beside his chair and put a bottle on the table.

Part of the strength which enabled him to lead a mob was that, contrary to his reputation, he didn't pick a quarrel unless his interests were in danger and never refused to talk if his instinct told him business might be in the offing.

'Later, maybe later.'

'What's your racket, mate?'

'No racket.'

Flint adjusted his tie with its design seemingly based on the interior of an Amazon jungle.

'You got a mob – you got no racket?'

'No racket.'

Ron Flint stubbed out the wet end of his cigar and turned to his jacket hanging over the back of his chair and pulled another cigar from the breast pocket and began to peel off the wrapping, and said disapprovingly,

'You're gonner be in need of public assistance, you're gonner be a burden on the rates, you are, mate.'

'Want a word about Lawrence Brown.'

'Punk priest,' Flint said morosely, all the interest dying out of his eyes. 'He back or sumppen?'

'Not back. You ought to know.'

'Now see 'ere, Mr Subden—'

'Sugden. Yorkshire name.'

'I told you once already this evening—'

'I think he's dead,' Sugden said abruptly and saw the startled look in Ron Flint's eyes.

'Dead? What of?'

Sugden waved his hand vaguely.

'Knife, bullet, blunt instrument – there's a lot of it about, they say.'

Ron Flint bit off the end of his cigar and spat it on the floor, saying nothing. Sugden pulled out a Stopper to fill the silence, 'Here today, gone tomorrow, as you might put it.'

Flint applied a match to his cigar. 'He ain't got a mob – who'd want to kill a punk priest, mate?'

'You,' said Sugden bleakly and drew a deep breath, 'you among others, since you ask.'

Sugden again saw the warning twitches on Ron Flint's face and remembered Tallow Hair's words, 'He'll slice you, Ron will,' and thought, well, they can do a lot with stitching these days and there's that place near Roehampton for skin grafts and things, and he knew he shouldn't have played it the way he had done.

He'd never been gone over by ordinary criminal thugs and wondered almost subconsciously whether it hurt, or whether in the turmoil, the thumping and grunting and obscenities and gasps and sheer physical struggle, the woundings hurt at first or only later; and the thought-flashes and tensing of his muscles seemed to have played tricks with his hearing because Ron's voice seemed to be travelling and echoing down a long tunnel, like down a subway, like the subway where the Small Fry had tried to do him.

'You don't want to say things like that, not without your mob with you, or even with your mob with you, not to me, not to me, mate. Why would anybody want to knock off the punk priest? Don't make sense, mate.'

Sugden swallowed, and was ashamed to realise that it was a nervous reaction based on relief.

'Secrets. Confessional. He knew too much. All right while he was a priest. Lips sealed. Not now, not now he's an atheist. Lips not sealed. Get it?'

Ron Flint banged the table so hard with his fist that one of the beer-bottles lurched. Sugden steadied it and heard Ron Flint say hoarsely in a voice hardly above a whisper, 'I never confessed nothing to incriminate nobody,' and when Sugden had worked out the three negatives in one short sentence he looked Flint in the eyes and intuitively believed him, and said so.

'But will the boys?' Sugden added mildly, and nodded towards the door.

Instantly, the same kind of look came into Ron Flint's eyes as he had noted when Tallow Hair thought he was bluffing to get rid of Ernie in the subway – crafty, knowing, half-admiring. Ron Flint nodded.

'Got no real racket, you don't need one, do you, mate?'

'Meaning?'

'Come off it, mate. Meaning blackmail, mate, meaning I got to pay you off to keep your trap shut, meaning you want to cut in here, on my patch, that's what you mean. Nothin' doing, mate.'

Sugden placed his hands palms down on the red table-cloth and leaned forward and said earnestly,

'Don't want to cut in on your patch, Mr Flint. Just want your help. Father Lawrence Brown was scared, dead scared. He knew too much, he knew he knew too much. He needed money, he was possibly going to emigrate before the book came out, change his name, disappear, start life afresh, who knows? Maybe he was, maybe he wasn't.'

'Let the silly bastard go,' Ron Flint said sourly.

'I think Father Brown has gone – for good. I think he's dead,' he repeated.

'You *are* a cop, then?'

'Not a cop. Government, but not a cop. You haven't thought it through, have you? I think Father Brown has been what you might call permanently sealed off, him and his secrets, and I think Mavis will be permanently sealed off. There's a lot of it going around, as I said.'

'Like what?' Ron Flint asked, sitting very still and staring at Sugden.

'Like cement. Like taking a swim in the Thames in a cement overcoat, as the saying goes. Like that, see? Maybe he told her nothing but they may not believe it, they won't want to risk it, not if the secret is big enough, will they, well, will they?'

'They, they, they, who's *they*?' Ron Flint said irritably.

'Excuse me saying it,' replied Sugden loudly, one hand holding his forehead, 'but that's a daft question, daft as a bloody brush. I wouldn't be here if I bloody well knew, would I? I'd be at home in bloody bed, wouldn't I?' He added more calmly, 'They might be Dutch, Czechs, Belgians, Russians, bloody Bulgarians, French, Germans, Italians, meaning Mafia, Chinese, Japanese, or Eskimos, and they might be in drugs, prostitution, gambling, spying, horse doping, greyhound nobbling – you name it, your guess is as good as mine.

'But this is a dead cert, and dead's a nasty word at the moment: they're a big mob, a bloody big mob, lad, able to keep observation on him every day, aye, even in Portugal. Getting to know his habits, his routines, if any, so's they could seal him off permanently, like I said, seal him off quickly if the order came.'

Sugden paused, then said slowly,

'He spotted something, of course, bound to in the end, but he didn't know what it was. He may even have thought it was our mob keeping a fatherly eye on him in view of what he knew, but I don't think so. He was scared, worried and scared. *And then the order did come.* I think it may come about Mavis.'

Ron Flint scratched the back of his head. A thought

was crossing his mind. It was a short enough journey. Then it recrossed.

'Why her?'

'Same reason. They don't know if he told her anything or nothing, a little or a lot. They wouldn't like doubts like that. They'll want to seal her off, one way or another, close her mouth, and I think there's only one way. Sorry, Mr Flint, I know—'

'You can call me Ron,' said Ron Flint grudgingly.

'I know she means something to you, she's got her own ways but—'

'She's got class, but no "form" – no record, never been "inside".'

'She's got class,' lied Reg Sugden and nodded. If Ron Flint thought she had class then it was all right as far as he was concerned. Originally he had wanted to use her to take him to Ron Flint and his mob on a friendly basis because the Flint mob had as good a chance as anybody else of picking up whispers about the ex-priest.

Now it wasn't necessary. He was getting on all right with Flint. And now, the more he thought of it, the more her safety was becoming a burden on what he always referred to as his 'shrivelled bit of leather', meaning what remained of his conscience.

The stratagem of the tethered goat attracting the tiger so that he, brave Sugden, could then deal with the tiger just wasn't on. He had been leaning too heavily on air. She would have to go back north to Newcastle. But arranging that would take a little time.

Meanwhile, what? He knew his own lot wouldn't spare much manpower for the sake of a theory. Ironically, there was only one crowd who might help.

'Get your boys to keep an eye on the place at night,' he said to Ron Flint, 'get the small fry to do it, make 'em feel important, useful, don't tell 'em why, just tell 'em to knock off anybody lurking about, except policemen, of course. Don't tangle with the cops.'

'Boring,' said Ron Flint doubtfully. 'They won't like it.'

'Only for two or three nights. Who's boss here?'

'There's only one. Me.'

Sugden left it at that. But he said,

'What about tonight? There's a hole in her basement window a yard wide. Somebody threw a brick through it. Anybody could get in.'

'Thieves don't like climbing over jagged glass,' said Ron Flint authoritatively. 'And that's a fact. I know.'

'I'm not talking about thieves.'

Ron Flint thought for a moment. 'I'll have new glass and bars put in tomorrow. I know a local bloke who can put in bars as quick as kiss my backside – and remove them, too, come to that,' he added thoughtfully.

'A nut-case with a brown dog living opposite chucked the brick.'

'Oh, him,' muttered Ron Flint contemptuously. 'I know him. He's a nut about religion, that's all. I'll have a word with him. Silly old bastard. He does little jobs for me sometimes.'

'And for who else?' asked Sugden bleakly, feeling the acid of his worry etching into his mind and soul. He pointed at a table in the corner of the room and the telephone standing on it.

'Tonight might be dicy for her. Give her a ring now. Tell her I'm with you. Tell her one of the boys will pick her up and she's to bring some things for the night. They can fix her up with a bed here – if *you* ask them.'

He watched Ron Flint hesitating.

'Windy, Mr Subden?'

'Sugden. Not windy. Bit anxious.'

Ron Flint shrugged and went to the phone and dialled a number.

Sugden watched him, listening to the unanswered ringing tone.

'Perhaps she's in bed,' he said at length.

'The phone's by her bedside,' muttered Ron Flint.

'You should know,' Sugden said.

After two or three minutes Ron Flint replaced the receiver.

Sugden said hopelessly,

'Not anxious, Ron. Windy, now, like you said. Windy.'

CHAPTER 11

When Reg Sugden had gone, Mavis Bailey carefully locked and bolted the door, humming some little-known verses about Cushie Butterfield, that voluptuous and famous lady. Then she went back into the living-room and switched on the television for the late-night news, saw nothing of interest, heard nothing of interest, and switched it off – and then did hear something of interest.

She hadn't pinned a blanket over the smashed window because the night was not cold and what she heard was a tinkle of glass from the front room.

She froze, and heard another tinkle, and assured herself that the falling glass was not glass which had been knocked out of the frame but some remaining pieces loosened by a passing car or by a tremor caused by the nearby Underground trains, because that is the kind of explanation one flies to.

When she heard nothing more except some faint music from a nearby house she decided that she might as well remove any more loose glass, and while she was about it she would, after all, pin a blanket across the window; so she went to a cupboard and took out an old blanket, and then a hammer and some tacks, and walked quickly and firmly into the front room and up to the broken window, and gasped, and felt the tingle of goose-flesh racing down her neck and spine as she looked up and saw the bottom half of a pair of uncreased trousers and the broad spade-shaped head of a brown dog staring down at her from the pavement.

Instinctively she gripped the hammer tighter and banged it on the window ledge, and heard her own voice above the faint, distant music,

'Get to hell out of it, you miserable old devil!'

Instantly the trouser-legs moved along the pavement and the dog's head, jerked by a lead, moved with the legs, but after going a couple of yards the legs and the dog stopped. Mavis was about to shout more expletives and a few obscenities when she heard the sound of a vehicle drawing up in front of the house-steps and looked out and saw a blue van-type vehicle with a notice on the side saying POLICE and a blue lamp on the roof, and immediately the dog's head jerked again and the dog and its owner moved quickly on and out of sight.

The young uniformed officer apparently must have seen the white blob of her face and he ran down the basement steps to the window and said quietly,

'Your name Bailey, miss? Mavis Bailey?'

She nodded silently, savouring her relief.

'You had a bit of trouble? A Mr Sugden phoned us and asked us to call round. Something to do with a brick?'

The police officer stared at the smashed window. She nodded and pointed up the street to her left.

'He did it!' she said excitedly. 'Fella with a brown dog, walking up the street there, you pull him in, he did it! Old swine, damned old swine! You pull him in, he lives opposite, pull him in before he gets into his house and goes to bed and cooks up some bloody silly alibi, that's him, grab him!'

'You want to charge him, miss?'

''Course I want to charge him!'

The officer nodded, glanced up at the pavement above, hesitated a second, then said,

'He'll need more than a phoney alibi, miss, if what

Mr Sugden said is correct. You still got the note which was round the brick?'

'Too true I have.'

He nodded briskly and jerked his head towards another man standing by the area steps dressed in civilian clothes, and said,

'Dabs, here, he wants to try for fingerprints, see? Don't handle the note more than you need or have done.'

He turned and went to the basement door. In the bright light of the living-room she handed the plain-clothes man the note, holding it gingerly by one corner, and watched him take out his box of tricks and select a soft camel-hair brush and a squat bottle of powder and a magnifying glass, and take everything over to a table near the door.

She looked at the uniformed officer, with his blue eyes and fresh complexion and rather old-fashioned short, neat haircut, and thought, they're not bad to look at, some of the fuzz, better than Larry, and in a clean, healthy way better than Ron, and in fact if it hadn't been for Ron she might have had a crack at him. Just for kicks, of course.

'There's three lots,' said the plain-clothes man looking round.

'There would be, wouldn't there,' Mavis said, 'mine, Reg Sugden's and that old swine's opposite.'

The officer nodded and said, 'Home and dry, if you ask me. We'll do him all right.'

'Nut-case,' said Mavis.

'The court will give him one month, suspended sentence, and a packet of ten fags,' muttered the officer morosely. 'I'll need a signed statement from you, miss, and more of your own fingerprints – perfect ones – for elimination purposes.'

She began to move towards the plain-clothes man but

the officer said, 'Not here, miss. Old Dabs and his box of tricks, he's just for discovering fingerprints, miss. For permanent stuff we've got sort of ink-pads at the station, and we press your fingers down on one of them, and that's that. And we can take your statement at the same time, more or less.'

He looked at her and smiled and she thought she might have a go at him anyway, Ron or no Ron, circumstances permitting.

He said, speaking carefully,

'We'll run you round there, and perhaps you might bring your night-clothes, miss.'

'Night-clothes?' she queried, and thought of her previous speculation – might have a go at him, Ron or no Ron, just for kicks, circumstances permitting. Perhaps they might be permitting. He continued to smile at her.

'Night-clothes, miss. This Mr Sugden, he's been on to somebody in Whitehall, who's been on to our Chief Superintendent. This Mr Sugden, he seems worried about your safety and you spending the night here till some bars are put on the window. We can put you up for the night, miss.'

'In a cell?'

He laughed. 'No, miss, there's some police sleeping accommodation above the station.'

If she had a guardian spirit he must have been absent without leave, or at least late on parade. 'Okay,' she said, and went quickly into the bedroom and put pyjamas and toilet necessities into a little hold-all, thinking that Reg Sugden had been right when he said that he could look after her better in London than in Newcastle.

'Well, miss, we'll go along,' the officer said when she came back into the room. But as he opened the door in the living-room the 'phone-bell began ringing.

She hesitated, then went towards the bedroom saying,

'It's probably my friend Ron. I think he rang before, just before you arrived. I didn't answer, being in the loo. He rings around midnight to see if I'm O.K. I'll tell him to keep it short.'

She went into the bedroom and lifted the receiver and instead heard Sugden's voice asking if she was all right.

' 'Course I'm all right,' she said loudly, because there was no guardian voice to tell her otherwise. There was a pause, then she heard him say,

'Look, Ron's worried about you sleeping there, and so am I, come to that. Ron'll fix you up with a bed in the pub—'

She interrupted him, not wanting Ron to come lumbering round to cart her off for the night in a frowsy old pub, far preferring the prospect of accommodation above the police station, just for one night, and first a matey hour with the blue-eyed officer, making out her statement. Then a cup of tea, perhaps, and more chat, and then a warm bed. And maybe if he had an hour off duty during the night he could slip up and see if she was all right.

So as the guardian spirit was still absent, she interrupted Sugden impatiently, her tone angry,

'Tell Ron to stop fussing.'

She put down the receiver and remembered she'd forgotten to tell Sugden that she knew already he was still worried because the police had told her so, and it was kind of him.

She would have added that it gave her a warm, cosy feeling to feel protected and know that he cared about her. Yes, she would have said that, because she might meet him again some time, and she wouldn't mind an evening with Reg Sugden, Ron or no Ron. He had his own kind of attraction, not blue eyes and a good figure, but brown eyes and the figure rather bulky – well, sturdy, strong-looking, and the beginnings of sideboard whiskers he was trying to make trendy, and a slight Yorkshire accent.

She thought of ringing him back, as he was obviously with Ron, but decided against it because there was no guardian voice to insist that she should. But there was the policeman, not the dowdy, bespectacled, fingerprints man, but the officer. She went back into the living-room thinking life could be fun if you knew how to play the system, and there were all sorts of lovely men around if you knew how to play *them* and took your chances when they occurred.

She gave no thought at all to Larry Brown. She had already decided that if he returned she would play it from there; and if he didn't, then he didn't. Most of the fun was in catching the fish. Eating it was good at first but the taste always palled in the end. Even Ron Flint would have palled if she had eaten him all the time, but she hadn't and wouldn't because there were periods when he was away enjoying the hospitality of Her Majesty's prisons.

'O.K.,' she said again when she was back in the living-room, and scribbled something on a buff envelope. She began to switch off the lights but stopped by the outer door and said, 'Perhaps I ought to get a thicker overcoat?' but the policemen were obviously anxious to be on their way, and said it was warm at the station and anyway they could always lend her a good thick overcoat if she needed one.

If she could have read his thoughts as he stood there, tall and elegant and fresh-looking, she would have read, 'You're going to be given a thicker overcoat than you bargain for, Little Miss Priest's Bird.' But there was nobody about, visible or invisible, to translate his thoughts for her. On the contrary, the immediate future looked bright and promising, at least for the night.

★   ★   ★

She licked the gum on the buff envelope and stuck it on the basement door and the policeman shook his head disapprovingly.

'You don't want to leave notes like that to the milkman, miss, it invites burglars. Insurance companies don't like it.'

She shrugged.

'I'm not insured.'

'You should be. But you're a bad risk, I suppose.'

'Why?'

She was vaguely puzzled. She had heard the words at some time, and some time very recently, but in the general movement as she fumbled for her keys and double locked the door there was no time for ordered thought or disciplined attempts to search her memory. Maybe somebody somewhere was back on guardian duty at last and trying to get through. If so, the line was out of order, and anyway it was too late. Nevertheless, she said again,

'Why?'

'Dicy neighbourhood,' murmured the policeman, 'especially now, of course.' He gestured towards the smashed window. 'You want to get that repaired quick, and with bars, too.'

'Yes, yes, that's right, I will,' she said as they went up the basement steps and walked to the police van.

Another police officer was sitting at the wheel, she saw, and he leaned forward and opened the side door, and she watched Dabs climb in and move to a long seat at the back, apparently because the front passenger-seat was cluttered up with some tools and small spare-parts. She followed him and sat beside him and the blue-eyed officer climbed in and sat on her other side.

The seat stretched from one side of the van to the other and was roomy enough for four people if necessary. There were no side windows. It was a big van with several feet of room between the front seats and the big rear one. The back seat was on long runners and could be moved forward away from the rear doors, and she thought inconsequentially that in its time the van had probably hauled off its fair quota of street demonstrators. But they'd probably been travelling on the floor-boards.

As the officer made his way to the back she heard him say irritably, 'What's all this doing here?' and heard him stumble over some obstacle dumped by the side. 'Lady might have tripped and hurt herself,' he muttered. And now, unexpectedly, a fourth man appeared, and moved the tools off the front seat by the driver and climbed in.

She saw he was wearing civilian clothes and an old-fashioned, trilby-style hat, but she took no further notice of him except to acknowledge his brief greeting with a murmured 'Good evening'. He was too old to be interesting to her.

'He's our inspector,' the officer whispered. 'Been keeping an eye on the place while we were inside.' She nodded indifferently.

The driver started the engine and engaged the clutch and the van moved forward, and she saw reflected in passing windows the flashing of the blue bulb on the roof.

As she had come up the steps and walked to the van she had noticed behind the van another vehicle, a dark, powerful-looking car she had never seen outside the houses before. And as the engine of the police van fired into life she heard the engine of the car behind starting.

The officer put his arm along the back of the seat behind her and rested his hand lightly on her right shoulder. She leant very slightly against it, a movement which, if not strong enough to be provocative, at least was not discouraging. She said,

'What's the black car behind? It's following us. I can hear it change gear.'

'Extra precautions, miss,' the officer said, patting her shoulder, and she thought she heard the uniformed driver snigger.

'You're important. Centre of attention, miss,' the officer said in a tone which was almost bitter. 'Doesn't happen more than once or twice in a lifetime, perhaps; perhaps only once, perhaps not at all. You want to enjoy it while it lasts, miss.'

She remembered, fleetingly, Larry's last Mass, when he'd had things thrown at him and had stood Christ-like, arms extended. It had been one of her big moments. And his, too, she was sure of that. Now where was he? She shivered.

'I am enjoying it,' she said, and pressed a little closer to him. 'I'd enjoy it more if I wasn't so bleedin' cold, I should have brought my thick coat, like I said.'

She hoped he would draw her closer with his right arm but he didn't. He said,

'We'll give you a coat later, miss. Won't we, Fred?' He spoke more loudly so that the driver could hear. 'We'll give her an overcoat later, won't we, Fred?'

'A real thick one we will,' the driver said and sniggered again.

'Keep her warm, eh?'

'Keep her real warm. Proper wind-cheater, and water-proof, too, eh?' He laughed outright and she thought she felt a slight quiver on her left as though the officer had suppressed a laugh, and from her right came a sound as though Dabs, the fingerprint man, had choked a giggle.

'What's so bloody funny about this overcoat you talk about?' she asked suspiciously. The driver called Fred turned his head slightly, for a second.

'Nothing funny, really, miss. Nothing really funny, is there?'

Before the officer could reply Dabs, on her right, said,

'Itth jutht a bit 'spethal, mith.'

He had hardly spoken in the house and she now noted that he had difficulty in pronouncing his Ss, and spoke in a whining muffled voice.

She sat up and looked at him. 'What's special about it?'

'Itth kept for spethal people, mith. Very important people, V.I.P.s, mith, like you.'

'What's the joke, then?' she insisted.

The officer patted her right shoulder and said soothingly,

'Just a local kind of joke, miss.'

The driver called Fred said, 'Family joke you could call it, miss. It's just that when this coat's been used it's always seemed a bit small, somehow.'

'Bit tight wound the hipth,' agreed Dabs, who also had trouble in pronouncing his Rs.

'Bit tight round the hips,' agreed the officer. 'But warm.'

'Warm and weatherproof,' Fred said.

'Windpwoof,' said Dabs.

'Warm, wind and wainproof, mith,' said Fred, imitating Dabs's muffled, whining voice, and they all laughed again, including Dabs.

Mavis Bailey said suddenly, 'Which police station are we going to?'

She knew one or two, having visited them, usually with a lawyer, when Ron Flint had been absent-minded or careless. They had crossed the river and she knew they were going down Elizabeth Street.

'Gerrard Road, Chelsea, miss,' said Fred.

'We've passed it,' she said sharply. 'We've just passed it.'

The officer beside her coughed and said, 'He means Kensington Police Station, Earls Court Road, miss.'

She said nothing but now sat bolt upright. The officer said, 'You don't look comfortable, miss.'

'I'm not.'

'Try leaning back, miss.'

'I'm thinking.'

'You could think leaning back, miss.'

'Not these thoughts, I can't.'

Nor could she, yet she did not know what she was thinking, or what thoughts she was pursuing or should be pursuing. She only knew that she felt uneasy and was in fact hurriedly trying to find a reason for her unease, which in a way made it worse.

She felt sure the unease was caused by something Sugden had said or something she had read in the newspapers, or possibly both, and there was something the officer had said which fitted in somewhere; and she was trying to reconstruct her conversation with the officer when something clicked and she shivered again.

She had said she wasn't insured and he had said, 'You should be. But you're a bad risk, I suppose,' and Reg Sugden, earlier, had said Larry was a bad insurance risk because he knew too much, and even if he never spilled the beans they wouldn't risk it, whoever they were, and that the same thing in a way applied to her. They might try and seal him off, as he called it, and seal her off, too.

Yet it was silly, she told herself, not daring to look at the possibilities, it was a police van and these were friendly cops and they were taking her to safety and a good night's sleep.

'And anyway Larry didn't tell me anything,' she told herself, aloud, absent-mindedly, staring at the road ahead through the windscreen. She felt the officer stiffen.

'What might he have told you, miss?'

'Oh, nothing. Skip it.'

He didn't press her further. They had driven to Sloane Square and along Sloane Avenue and past South Kensington Underground station, and had cut up and across

Cromwell Road, and were approaching the traffic lights at the corner of Kensington High Street and Kensington Church Street. It seemed a long way round but perhaps more straightforward than across country via Marloes Road and Scarsdale Villas. She couldn't remember.

It was when they were held up at the bottom of Kensington Church Street that a street lamp made the interior of the van slightly less dark and she saw what the officer had complained about when he had stumbled over something in the back of the van as he made his way to the back seat.

He had stumbled over two large, white, bulging bags lying on their sides on one side of the van. There was print on the backs of the bags, impossible to read easily in bad lighting but one of the bags had tilted sideways a little so that part of the large lettering on the front was visible, and she made out some of the top word, -TISH, which was probably part of BRITISH, and the third word ended -PANY, and was probably COMPANY, and both words were dull enough, and so was the word above, between BRITISH and COMPANY.

That word too was dull enough in the normal way because nothing is more dull than cement, and she could make out -EMENT, and the last part of the letter C and for a few seconds BRITISH CEMENT COMPANY and its products rang no alarm-bells in her mind at all. But when the bells did start ringing they jangled one after another in quick succession, building up to a crescendo of panic which mingled with the sound of her heart thumping in her ears.

The first alarm-bell was set off by recollections of both Sugden and the officer telling her she was a bad insurance risk; and the second bell, rambling, confused and less clear, concerned bits she had read in newspapers about people being enclosed in cement and dropped in rivers or the sea. The third and final bell, loudest and clearest of all because it touched on more recent events, was the obscure joke which had so amused these men a moment or two ago.

The 'local joke', the 'family joke'.

The laughs and sniggers about giving her a warm overcoat. Weatherproof. Rainproof. A bit small, a little 'tight wound the hipth'.

She knew she had to keep her head if she were to evolve some way of getting out of the van, if she could, if she ever could. She had to seem normal if she could, if she could. She practised some words in her mind and took a deep breath so that when she spoke her voice would come out strongly, without a tremor. She said,

'Funny old van, innit?' and she pointed at the wide floor-space between the back seat and the front seats.

'Just an ordinary old utility van, miss,' said the man she still thought of as a police officer.

'Used for this and that,' said Fred.

'Like picking up drunks and dumping them on the floor.'

'Uthed for all thorth of thingth. You'd be thurpwithed, mith.'

Each in turn added to the double-meanings and once more they all laughed, Fred loudly and harshly, the officer softly, more with his body than his voice-box, and Dabs gave his usual snuffly giggle.

Her fear made her mind acute and now that she could catch the second meaning of their words she could understand why they were amused, and felt the palms of her hands growing damp.

She laughed herself, politely, glad that there was no tremor in the laugh because what she had to do, or rather, try to do, was better done in a well-lit High Street like Kensington. Or perhaps not? There was no question of jumping out. There were double doors behind her but she guessed they were locked.

'I said something funny?' she asked. 'Family joke or something?'

'It's complicated, miss,' said Fred, half turning his head. 'We'll tell you later.'

'In an hour or so,' said the officer-type.

'You'll laugh then, mith. You weally will, mith! Laugh your head off, mith!' She hated Dabs the most.

Just past the Kensington Church Street traffic lights she put her hand on her stomach and then on her mouth and said,

'I feel a little queasy, officer.'

'It's the thtwain, mith.'

'That's right, the strain of the evening, you'll feel better soon,' the officer said. 'Open the driver's window, Fred, the lady's feeling a bit queasy.'

The driver wound down his window and said,

'It'll soon pass.'

'Soon pass,' agreed the officer. 'Be over in an hour or so. When you've got a chance to rest, miss.'

'When you've a chance to wetht,' said Dabs and sniggered again.

At the pedestrian-crossing lights, just beyond the Underground station, she said,

'I don't feel up to going to the police station. I'll come tomorrow. I want to get out. I'll get a taxi back.'

The officer-type patted her shoulder.

'You don't want to get out and start wandering around looking for a taxi at this time of night, miss. London ain't as safe as it used to be, not at night it ain't, not for young ladies like you, miss. You sit back, we'll soon be there, we'll look after you when we're at the station.'

She didn't sit back· but, on the other hand, she didn't repeat the request to get out, or say it would be pretty

170

safe in Kensington High Street. She sat looking straight ahead and once she wiped the sweat off the palms of her hands, rubbing them quickly across her knees, and looked at the bags of cement on the van floor, yet also thinking of the laughs she had heard, and how kind they seemed. Perhaps she was wrong. She decided to do nothing until they reached the traffic lights a few hundred yards further on, at the corner of Earls Court Road. But what then?

They should turn left at the lights and the police station, she knew, was a few hundred yards down the Earls Court Road on the right.

There is a natural instinct to cling to the normal, the mundane, the expected, and she saw no harm in waiting to see if they turned left at the traffic lights. It was only a question of waiting a minute or two.

If they turned left her immediate fear would be allayed, would seem over-dramatic, childish, even ridiculous.

The traffic lights turned red and they slowed down, and she noted that although the left-hand traffic lane was clear, where they should be in order to turn left, they were in the right-hand lane, and when the lights turned green they moved straight ahead.

'You should have turned left for Earls Court Road,' she said hopelessly. 'You should have turned left,' she repeated, 'for Kensington Police Station, in Earls Court Road.'

'We're actually going to Hammersmith,' the officer said soothingly. She said loudly, in an astonished voice,

'Not Gerrard Road station, like he said? Not Kensington, like you said he meant? Hammersmith now?'

'Old Fred gets confused. He doesn't know whether he's coming or going sometimes.'

'Or where he'th coming fwom or going to,' added Dabs and gave a high-pitched laugh.

She nodded, saying nothing, not moving, giving the appearance of being satisfied with the implication that Fred the police driver was apparently not only mentally retarded but positively moronic. As they were passing Olympia on the right she said sharply,

'I want to get out now. I'll make my own way back, like I said.'

Fred turned his head.

'You don't want to get out, miss. Why do you think you want to get out?'

'I feel sick, like I said.'

'It'll pass, like *we* said.'

'No it won't. I feel sick, I'm going to be sick. Stop the van.'

When the van did not slow down she repeated in a loud voice, trying to sound commanding, even imperious,

'Stop the van, I say! Stop it now!'

She leaned forward from her seat automatically, without any hope, to make for the left, nearside door. Fred the driver turned his head. He said,

'She getting restless, comrade?'

'Very restless, comrade,' the officer said.

'Werry wethtleth indeed, comwade,' muttered Dabs.

'Tape,' said Fred crisply, and she felt the officer's right arm come round her shoulders while his left hand groped for and found her wrists, and he pulled her back and held her while Dabs sniggered and fought to put adhesive tape over her lips and round her wrists, murmuring, 'Don't thtwuggle, mith. I might hurt you with the thitherth ath I cut the tape.'

But she did struggle and also began to scream, wondering how much of her screaming would reach the world outside the van, and if any reached the outside world, what the passing outside world would think. Another drunk being carted to the cells? A drug-addict nearly out of her mind? And the outside world shrugging its collective shoulders, minding its own business, unable and very unwilling to interfere, would go on its way.

She twisted her head from side to side as she screamed, and wriggled and wrenched, and once managed to free her hands and wrists and even lurch towards the driver with some idea of making him crash the van. And all the time she screamed and swore.

But there could be only one end, and there was, and they tipped her forward to the floor and she lay there, trussed and silent.

She lay there with her back against one of the bags of cement from the British Cement Company, thinking of cement overcoats and death.

CHAPTER 12

After Mavis had hung up on him Sugden put down the
receiver and looked at Ron Flint.

'She's playing silly. She doesn't want to come. I've a
feeling she's with somebody.'

'I'll give her playing silly,' Ron Flint said and opened
the door and shouted at the landlord in the bar, 'Rammy-
boy, make up a bed for a lady tonight.'

He didn't wait for a reply. Rammy-boy always did what
he was told, not wanting to have a lot of glass and bottles
broken by mistake on purpose. Flint turned to Sugden.

'We'll go and pick her up. Silly little cow.'

Sugden nodded. 'In your car. Mine's not easy to drive
at the moment. As you know,' he added sourly. 'As you
bloody well know, don't you?'

Ron Flint met his gaze, eyes hard in sallow, rubbery
face, and straightened his Amazon jungle tie.

'Bit of a mistake. Sorry.'

Because he might need him, Sugden met him half-way
with a Stopper. 'Happen in the best regulated families,
mistakes,' he murmured.

Flint said, 'I'll get it repaired. My mob will do it.'

'Not as fast as mine.'

'Want to bet on it?'

Sugden reflected and said, 'No.'

'Pick it up here tomorrow night, let's go.'

Ten minutes later they were looking at the buff envelope
on her door, and the untidy, awkward lettering: 'Milk-

man. No milk for three days please.' There was no reply when they rang the bell.

Three minutes later Mr Benjamin Harris, opposite, shouted, 'Sit down yer silly—!' and swiped at the spade-shaped head of his brown dog. He had come down in response to the door-bell.

He was wearing a dilapidated old dressing-gown, the same colour as his dog, and was standing shivering on his front door-step.

Sugden pushed him inside and against a wall in the hall and held him there with his chest, staring into the watery blue eyes with his own hostile dark ones.

Behind him the brown dog growled.

'Shut yer gob,' said Mr Harris. 'Old dog doesn't like strangers,' he explained wheezily, back to the hall wall, trying ineffectually to push Sugden away from his chest.

Sugden smacked him gently across the left cheek. There was no force behind the blow, it was hardly more than a pat to help him concentrate his thoughts. He said,

'Where is she? Where's the priest's woman?'

'In hell, I hope! Old dog always growled when he saw her, old dog did, he knows, he knows papists and papists' whores when he sees 'em, old dog does. She's gone, and the devil's welcome to her!'

Flint was shorter than Sugden. It is possible that Harris did not know Flint was there until he heard his voice, sharp and peremptory, coming from behind Sugden's back.

'What happened, you silly bloody old image, what happened?'

Ron Flint shoved Sugden aside and glared at Harris and pulled a flick-knife out of his pocket and added, 'If that dog bites me it's his last bite. What happened?'

'Gone, Mr Flint, gone with the cops. I've flushed 'em

out, both of them, them and their plotting, wrote to the Home Secretary, I did, and to Her Gracious Majesty to make sure. She knows she can trust old Ben, she does, often write to Her Gracious Majesty, I do, and the cops came, like I knew they would—'

'What cops?' Sugden asked softly.

'What cops?' repeated Ron Flint equally softly, as though he was speaking to a child. 'Tell us what happened, Ben, tell us quickly.'

'Shut the door, Mr Flint, it's cold.'

'Keep it open,' Sugden said. 'Cool him down.'

Sugden's words sparked off Ron Flint. He said,

'Want to sit on ice, Ben? Ten, fifteen, thirty minutes, there's plenty at the pub. Rammy-boy keeps some for me. Leaves no marks, Ben.'

Ben Harris licked his lips.

'Not keeping nothing from you, Mr Flint. Half an hour or so ago I was out airing the old dog, see?'

'Again?' said Sugden. Harris affected to ignore him.

'Last walk of the night, Mr Flint. Always take the old dog out last thing. Once round the block and then in, whether he has or hasn't, dog's got to know who's master—'

'Shilly-shallying,' said Sugden. 'Playing for time.'

'Boxin' and coxin',' said Ron Flint. He moved away, saying, 'I'll get the lads to take him for a cold squat on the ice.' He turned back as Harris said,

'It was round the corner, the police van. They picked me up and chucked me inside, old dog and all, on to the floor. One of them, he started to go over me a bit, see? He said, "Had a complaint about you, you old bastard," he said. "Chucking a brick through a window." "Never done it," I said. "Was eatin' me tea at the time." "How do you know what time it was?" he says. "Heard a crash," I says, "went out to have a look." "Nuts," he says, "we're going

to charge you," he says, "unless you work your passage."
"Meaning?" I asks.'

He stopped and looked at Ron Flint with his watery blue
eyes, and sniffed.

'Like you always say, Mr Flint, help the police in small
things, you say, because you never know. No squealing,
of course, but be civil and helpful in what doesn't matter,
you say.'

Flint nodded. 'What did they want? Make it sharp and
make it true.'

' "Want a talk with Mavis Bailey," the cop says. "Go
ahead," I says, "what's stopping you, what's more natural,
her having a busted window, why not?" "Nah," he says,
"nah, nah. Want a private talk, nobody hanging around,
quick but private, about her priest boyfriend. Walk the
old dog up and down," he says. "Slip down the basement
steps, knock a few more bits of glass out, and nip up and
see what happens. She'll be scared, of course, but she'll
come to the window, and if she's with anybody she'll bring
him with her, her being scared. If she's alone, stand by
the basement with the old dog, looking down. Then we'll
drive up and you can walk away, see?"

'So I said, "Well, okey-doke, but I don't get it," I said.
"You don't need to," he says. "It's better you don't." So
I did.'

His voice trailed away and he pulled his dressing gown
closer.

'Can I go back to bed?'

'No,' Sugden said. Flint said,

'What sort of van was it?'

'Ornery police job – blue light on top.'

'Notice the number?' asked Sugden without hope.
Harris shook his head mournfully, then suddenly his blue
eyes blazed with their fire of mental instability.

'I bin framed,' he muttered fiercely. 'That's what I've bin. Framed.'

Sugden looked at him pityingly.

Flint asked, 'How framed?'

'Note in an envelope under my door this morning,' Harris replied in the same fierce muttering voice. But his eyes had clouded over and he seemed to be trying to think something through to a conclusion which he could slot into his fanaticism.

Flint shook him roughly. 'What did the note say?'

'Note said, "Top secret. Chuck a brick through the Romish Priest's window this evening nine-ish and your battle's won Home Secretary says and top secret destroy this." All in capital letters it was. So I did. I bin framed,' he muttered yet again, eyes once more hot and angry. 'They're all in it, Home Secretary, the lot.'

He paused, then raised his head and when he spoke his own secret pride, mythical and self-perpetuating, which lent a reason to his drab life, sounded clear and vibrant in his tone. 'But Her Gracious Majesty knows she can rely on old Ben to beat the Papists in the end – she knows, *she knows!*'

Sugden said,

'O.K., you can get back to bed.'

Harris sniffed and went up the stairs, dragging his brown dog with him. Sugden and Ron Flint looked at each other.

'Bird's flown,' Flint said, adding in a shaky voice, 'real cops don't act like that. I should know.'

Sugden shook his head.

'Bird's not flown – bird's been netted.'

He looked at Ron Flint's face and reluctantly felt the faint stirring of what could almost pass for compassion. They were an odd pair, Flint and Mavis, and they had some odd habits, mostly anti-social, yet they seemed to be fond of each other.

They were marauders in the jungle, dangerous animals, best left alone by other animals; each marauder going separate ways, yet invariably uniting from time to time for mutual admiration and perhaps the affection which most animals occasionally need. Dangerous and totally merciless, like leopards or tigers; yet few people would enjoy the sight of even a man-eating tiger suffering. Thus Sugden tried to rationalise his flickering compassion for Flint.

Ron Flint licked his lips and said, 'What do we do?'

Sugden licked his own and said, 'I don't know. I'll have to get in touch with my office. But I don't know.'

'What office?'

Sugden ignored the question and Flint did not repeat it. Sugden looked at his watch. Some Underground trains would still be running. Just.

'Run me to the station, will you? My car being out of action. As you bloody well know,' he added harshly, the flickering compassion petering out for lack of gas.

At the station he went into a telephone kiosk and rang the night duty officer. The response was regretful and logical.

'Look, Reg, one police van looks like another, and if you haven't got the registration number I just can't ask the Metropolitan Police to run round like scalded cats, stopping each other's vans all over London at random, wrenching the back doors open, questioning and searching, it's not on, old boy, it's just not *on*. Blimey, there'd be civil war in the Met before dawn, and a good few casualties. Sorry.'

It was the sort of reaction he had expected and understood; yet he had hoped that, somehow, some idea might have cropped up. But nothing could be done on those lines, he saw that, and he replaced the receiver and took a train to Earls Court station, and walked down Earls Court

Road till he came to his own side-turning and the house where he had a flat.

He realised he hadn't eaten that evening and it was now past one o'clock in the morning. He poured himself a long whisky-and-soda and ate a hunk or two of cold mutton, a slice of cheese and some spring onions, and then went to bed, taking his burdened conscience with him, unable to throw off the sense of guilt, the knowledge that he had in effect persuaded Mavis to stay in London rather than go back up north; and she had agreed because he had told her she would be better protected down south than in Newcastle.

Now this had happened. She would have been safer anywhere than in her own flat.

He would have done something about her later but that evening all that he had managed to rustle up had depended on the goodwill of a local bully-boy and his gang of thugs. It was humiliating and worse. It hadn't been enough. Now they had picked her up to seal her off as they must have done the priest by now.

Froggy Vandoran was right, it wasn't a Fun Game, and he wondered about the nature of the secret which could cause so much deadly activity. But the speculation was a spin-off from his sense of guilt and responsibility and he was still worried and heavy-hearted when he climbed into bed.

As he lay in the dark he supplied himself with one of his own Stoppers, and thought, What's done is done and can't be undone, and his compartmentalised mind was such that in a few seconds he fell asleep and indeed slept very well; overslept, in fact, and arrived late at the office and found a note on his desk:

'Please have a word with Mr Vandoran urgently – 10.10 a.m.'

CHAPTER 13

He had a sickening feeling that he was going to hear bad news as he made his way to Vandoran's sunny room and knocked and entered and saw Vandoran sitting behind his big mahogany desk.

Whatever else might or might not be on the desk, there were always two objects. One was a short, vicious-looking Hitler Youth dagger in a black sheath bearing a small swastika, and on the other side of the desk was a small, framed photograph of the current head of the K.G.B.

Vandoran would say, if asked, or even if not asked, that these objects reminded him of his duty to keep a strict balance as between the intelligence services of the extreme Right and the extreme Left, though inevitably at certain stages of history, he would add, he was more concerned with one side than another.

Knowing what he himself now knew, Vandoran must have been well aware that Sugden was on edge. But Vandoran had an irritating habit of building up slowly to what he wanted to discuss.

It infuriated his staff and it infuriated Sugden now.

On entering the room Sugden had expected to see the usual wide, frog-like smile of greeting spread slowly across Vandoran's face. But there had been no smile, and there was no smile now.

'Take Napoleon,' Vandoran said and Sugden, putting a light to his pipe, said,

'You take him, I don't want him.'

'Napoleon prized one thing, almost above everything

else, in a general. A general might be intelligent, be brave, have initiative, but he had to have another quality. I take it you know what that was?'

'Yes, I do. He had to be lucky.'

'Napoleon had little use for a general unless he was lucky – or so I've been told. You are lucky.'

'Not from where I'm sitting,' Sugden said.

'You were lucky in Moscow, and lucky in Cyprus, and you are lucky now – so far. You are lucky because the Metropolitan Police, and most other police forces, are very touchy about their areas.'

'You needn't say that again.'

'Touchy about other forces intruding into their territories. It's the same in the animal and bird world,' Vandoran went on, eager to stress the similarity. 'Dogs urinate against lamp-posts to mark their domain, birds sing at least partly to indicate the bounds of their private estates, robins—'

'Yes,' Sugden said, 'yes, I know. Robin redbreasts are very fierce fighters, defending their territory. I know, I know.'

He tried to keep the impatience and irritability out of his voice.

Vandoran was at his worst, beating up to the point like a yacht tacking against the breeze, dragging in Napoleon, dogs, robins, the lot. It wasn't cat-and-mouse stuff because Vandoran bore no resemblance to a cat. It was frog-and-insect stuff, the frog half-submerged, watching amusedly, deciding when to spring.

'What did you wish to see me about?' Sugden asked woodenly, and glanced at his wristwatch.

'The van. The one you mentioned to the night duty officer. It had a number plate, and the registration letters indicated it was a Sussex County police van. One of the Met patrol cars saw it and wondered if etiquette had been observed, or if the Sussex vehicle was there on a little unannounced intrusion of its own. The patrol car passed the van and a black car following it, and signalled the van to draw in.

'In reply, the driver of the van flashed his headlights, pulled out and passed the patrol car, followed by the black saloon car. They both accelerated to a fast speed.

'This was downright rude, of course. Furthermore, the reply to an earlier routine radio query from the patrol car was coming in, and it showed that the van appeared to be using a false number-plate.

'Some thoughts about a possible bank robbery now occurred. It is not surprising. The Met car therefore switched on its siren and once more overtook the van and the black saloon – just after they had turned left down a narrow side-road. The patrol car halted twenty yards in front, and again signalled the van to draw in. This time it obeyed.

'The officers alighted, and as they walked back to the van the black saloon passed them and disappeared at a high speed. When they reached the van the driver was not there. Nor was there anybody in the passenger seats, either in front or behind. The black saloon, registration number noted but also untraceable, was clearly a fall-back escape vehicle for use in just such an emergency.

'Quite a well planned job on the whole,' added Vandoran thoughtfully. Sugden could have hit him.

'Empty, van abandoned,' Sugden said, his Adam's apple rising and falling twice as he swallowed. Vandoran said delicately,

'You should listen more carefully, it could be important on some occasions. I said nobody was in the driver's seat or on the passenger seats. But something was on the floor. I should have mentioned that. Something was on the floor behind, such as two sacks of cement. And your lady-friend, as you would have known before if you had got into the office a little more punctually.'

Vandoran was watching him, smiling smugly, and again Sugden could have thumped him. It had been a proper frog-and-insect ploy. But he was too breathless with relief to do or say anything. He listened vaguely as Vandoran said,

'Mouth taped up, of course. Ankles and wrists tied with tape, too – just as well, really. They had to move exceedingly quickly so they couldn't take an immobile woman with them.'

'Where is she?' muttered Sugden.

'In one of the safe houses.'

'Keep her there, keep her there.'

Vandoran nodded. 'I'll keep her there as long as it suits me.' He had taken the Nazi dagger out of its sheath and was bouncing the point up and down on the table. He said thoughtfully, 'I understand that when she had been released and had recovered a little your bird's north-country language was what you might call tasty, very tasty indeed. Especially about you.'

'She isn't my bird. Nor ever would have been.'

'If you can sell me that story you can sell a double-bed to the Pope of Rome,' Vandoran murmured coarsely.

'How long can she stay there?'

Vandoran frowned and thought, and the tattoo of the tip of the Nazi dagger on the table top increased its tempo.

'Three or four days, perhaps. Maybe a week.'

'And then?'

'She'll have to go out into the great big world again, won't she? We can't keep her indefinitely as a sort of grace-and-favour tenant, can we? She'll have to go. The world's full of people taking chances.'

'It's not full of people being kidnapped with a view to

certain assassination,' Sugden said bitterly. 'Most ransoms can be paid, if considered desirable or politic. This one can't. This ransom is silence – complete and final. And she's the only one who can pay it, and all she'll get by way of return is a one-way ticket to eternity. A poor bargain.'

Vandoran got up from his desk and began to walk up and down his room with his springy gait, short body rising and falling above his long legs.

'Imagine you're sitting with a powerful rifle on a raft,' he began, and Sugden groaned silently, knowing that Vandoran was about to indulge in one of his flights of imagery. 'You see the triangular fins of sharks swimming round, some near, some not. You should fire at the nearest one, not waste ammunition firing at them all. The others may devour it and be satiated, or be discouraged. If not, repeat the performance. Moral: don't try and solve all your difficulties at the same time. Most will solve themselves or disappear.'

'It's Mavis Bailey who'll disappear.'

In his practical Yorkshire way Sugden was not interested in theories, especially one involving a man on a raft who was surrounded by sharks and happened to have a rifle about him, thinking it would have been more handy if he had had a barrel of beer.

So he sat in his chair, chunky, brown-eyed and sullen, worried about Mavis and her future, but as he watched Vandoran return to his desk and try to smooth down the unruly quiff of hair which always sprouted from the crown of his head, he thought, reluctantly, He's a clever frog, Vandoran, he's switched the conversation from Mavis, and gained some time to think.

He added, 'All that's as may be, but we've shot nowt yet, and the only shark that has been scared off wasn't by us but by luck and a patrol car of the Met police.'

Vandoran had opened the file on his desk and was glancing at List 3, the people who might have been scared because they had confessed to the ex-priest, sufficiently scared to want to kill both him and the woman he ran away with.

'I take it we can rule out the town councillor, whether he has or hasn't been fiddling building contracts?'

Sugden nodded. 'He wouldn't have the organisation, anyway.'

'And this crook Flint?'

Sugden shook his head emphatically.

'They're a rum couple. He's a crook and she's got the morals of an alley-cat but they've got what you could call a kind of elastic faithfulness. They part and they come together again, and they know they will, and what one of them does when they are separated doesn't seem to worry the other. No fundamental jealousy, total self-confidence, because they know that when you get down to it each one has got the other by the—'

'Yes, I take your point.'

'He knows she would not have stayed with the priest long. He didn't need to kill him. And he'd never hurt the girl seriously, he might belt her round what is known in the vernacular as the lug-'ole, but nothing serious. Anyway, he, too, hasn't the organisation to lay on a show like last night. He's small, cheap stuff, thinks he's a big fish in a big pond, but he's a medium fish in a mini-pond.'

'Among the rest there's only one possible left, isn't there?'

'The Hon Member of Parliament?'

'Mr Edward Mallow,' said Vandoran.

Sugden took out a pocket-knife and began to scrape out the dottle in his pipe-bowl into an ash-tray on Vandoran's desk. It looked black and noisome, and Vandoran, who didn't smoke, watched with distaste. Sugden said,

'Frigging about round an M.P. is no joke. It's about as joky as stumbling over an uncharted minefield at night. Something'll blow up and whoops, away we go, questions in Parliament, official inquiry, the lot. So you'll have to watch it.'

'You mean *you'll* have to watch it,' Vandoran said smoothly.

Sugden looked up and shook his head.

'Not me, I'm not in that league.'

'You've just been promoted to that league.'

'What are you suggesting?' asked Sugden, and thought to himself, As if I don't know.

'As if you don't know,' said Vandoran, picking up Sugden's thought. 'I am saying that Mr Mallow, M.P. for ten years, keen member of a list of Parliamentary committees as long as your arm, having periodic access to secret information of a military, industrial, or political interest, is knowingly or unknowingly – but probably knowingly – willingly or unwillingly – but probably willingly – in the pay of a hostile intelligence service. And you know which one that is, or do I have to spell it out?'

Sugden nodded but he sighed and said, 'So much bloody work and what happens? Prison sentence of a few years, less one-third remission for good conduct. Later hailed as a hero-of-you-know-where and given the order-of-you-know-what. Over in you-know-where they kill them, and quite right, an' all.'

'I am going to kill Mallow,' said Vandoran simply.

Sugden looked and felt shocked.

'How?'

'Leave the details to me.'

'You must have proof,' muttered Sugden uneasily. 'Too much theory so far.'

'His death will provide the proof, if my theory is right.'

'If it isn't right, it'll be a bit late.'

187

Sugden got up to go but at the door he heard Vandoran call him back.

'You may be right, perhaps it's not your league, Reg.'

But Reginald Sugden turned and said,

'Maybe it is, after all. Traitors ought to be killed. A tribe must be protected. But how?'

'Leave the details to me,' Vandoran said again.

He was bouncing the tip of the Nazi dagger on his desk but his eyes were fixed on a framed picture of a Communist state labour camp. Then he stopped looking at the photograph of the labour camp and said, 'It's classic sacred cow trouble, except that it's a sacred bull, technically anyway. A perfect if extreme example of the protection of a sacred cow. You understand that?'

'No, I don't,' Sugden said flatly.

'Mallow is the sacred cow, regularly milked, and some of the milk is very creamy. Very creamy indeed. And still warm from the cow. Straight from the Parliamentary sub-committees and there's all the other fodder a Parliamentary sacred cow can feed on. Very savoury to the palate.'

He got up and did his usual frog-pacing round the room, feet turned outwards at a pronounced angle. He stopped by the window and stared out at the distant view of the Zoological Gardens and the angular silhouette of Lord Snowdon's aviary. When he turned his face towards Sugden, Sugden knew he wasn't thinking of him, or even seeing him.

The brown marble eyes seemed to be straining to obtain a more defined focus of something still partly obscured by mist.

The long thin lips were widely stretched but it was not at some amusing thought. Sugden was a very practical, worldly man but he nevertheless felt a touch of goose-flesh race over his skin. A loyal colleague, cunning, brave

188

and resourceful, and with a big machine at his disposal, Sugden thought. A terrible enemy. He was glad he was on Vandoran's side. He was even more glad when Vandoran's cold smile faded.

'I'm going to kill Mallow, the sacred cow,' Vandoran said again, forcing the words out, lips nearly closed.

Sugden smiled, politely.

'You can't kill an M.P.,' he said and tried to believe his own words.

'Who can't?'

'You can't. There'd be a question in the House.'

'There'll be questions in the House if I don't,' said Vandoran grimly. 'You see what's happening? There's this creamy milk. Maybe the best milk for a long time. They've got to protect it. I'd do the same. I'd kill, if need be.'

Sugden believed him. Vandoran might well do the same.

Vandoran was a concentrated force, not entirely of malignity, because in a way he was not devoid of humanity, provided it did not interfere with his work. He was a concentrated force of pure ferocity, easily misinterpreted as malevolence. Once again he felt glad he was on Vandoran's side; not that Vandoran invariably won his battles with foreign intelligence services. But he usually did.

Sugden heard him repeat, 'You see what's happening? They've sealed off Lawrence Brown the ex-priest and all he learnt in the confessional. They've sealed off Richardson, Mallow's close friend, who certainly knew too much, and Ernest Markham, Father Brown's publisher, in such a way that Lawrence Brown is obviously suspected of killing them both. And they would have sealed off Father Brown's woman but for a stroke of bad luck.

'Picked them off, one by one, so that only the sacred cow is left mooing in the meadow, alone and lonely, rich with their money but frightened, and more dependent on them than ever. By and large the operation has been well-executed – and executed is, if I may so, the proper word in the circumstances.'

He paused, then added, unsmiling, and in a deadly earnest tone,

'Only a sacred cow of unusual value would be worth an effort of that magnitude, and that is why—'

Again the tip of the Nazi dagger was beating a rapid tattoo on the desk. 'That is why I am going to kill him,' he repeated. 'What else can I do?'

'You could stop playing God,' suggested Sugden mildly. 'That's what you could do, stop playing God.'

Vandoran put down the dagger.

'God and I have our differences, that I admit, that I admit freely, but in matters of life and death and sacred cows He and I agree to a remarkable extent.'

Sugden often found it difficult to know when Vandoran was serious and when he was joking. On this occasion he knew that he was serious. He said,

'The woman Mavis Bailey is still at risk.'

Vandoran nodded. 'Inform her that we wish her to take advantage of our hospitality for a few days more. By that time it will be safe for her to venture into the world again, because by that time the sacred cow will be browsing on a type of grass not known on this earth. Come to think of it, why the delay? Tell her she will be safe by tomorrow – we hope.'

He glanced at a slip of paper and added,

'According to my information, Mr Mallow has booked in for a week at the Raleigh Hotel, near Marble Arch, until the police have finished in his flat and the mess has been cleared up. I would like you to call on him this evening.'

'No,' Sugden said sharply. 'No, I won't. Somebody else can do it. I won't.'

Vandoran gazed into Sugden's sullen, defiant face.

'You will, you know. You will if you know what's good for you. And I will come with you, I think I had better come with you.'

He pushed the slip of paper across the desk.

'There's his phone number. Ring him now, make an appointment for this evening. Say it is a matter of great importance to him which you can't discuss on the phone. Say you will call at nine-thirty, and a friend will be with you.'

Vandoran thought for a moment.

'Tell him – yes, if he demurs, tell him it is about Father Brown.'

'Names? Mine and yours?'

'Use our real names. And use this phone.'

Sugden looked bewildered.

'Our real names? On a killing job?'

'I told you to leave the details to me.'

Sugden shrugged, reached for Vandoran's telephone and dialled the number. When he had finished speaking and had replaced the handpiece, he said,

'He was reluctant at first.'

'I bet he was.'

'He thought for a long time, muttered about going to Durham tomorrow – and then agreed.'

Vandoran nodded happily, and said,

'It's not Durham he's going to.' Then, seeing the look on Sugden's face he added, 'You may set the remains of your conscience at rest. I shall not ask you to kill him. That responsibility will be mine. O.K.? Feel better?'

'Not much. I think you're mad, sir.'

He only called Vandoran 'sir' when he was worried.

Sugden could have got a message to Ron Flint that morning via Ramsden, the pub-keeper, saying that Mavis was safe, but he didn't. He thought he would let Flint sweat it out during the day. By the evening he would be more malleable.

Shortly after 6 p.m. when the pub opened, Sugden went in and went up to Flint, who was standing at the bar. Flint had kept his promise. The car was standing outside with a new windscreen and seats repaired. Some people had worked fast. Ron Flint handed him the keys and Sugden nodded and took them, and didn't say thank you. Flint was looking greyer even than usual, the lines of his rubbery face more deeply etched.

'Any news?'

'She's all right.'

Flint took a gulp of whisky and water.

'What the hell happened?'

Sugden gave an edited version of events.

'Where the hell is she?'

'Safe at the moment.'

Flint looked at his watch. 'I got a job later this evening. I'll pick her up now.'

'No, you won't. She's safer where she is.'

Sugden watched the grey in Flint's face slowly turn to pink and then red, and guessed that nobody in his local kingdom had spoken to him like this for a long time.

'I can protect her better at the moment. Like I did last night,' Sugden added shamelessly.

Flint banged his empty glass down.

'Cop, you're a cop, like I said.'

'Have another drink?'

'I don't drink with cops, mate. You oughter know that, mate.'

It was obviously a peculiarity of Flint that he never used the word mate when he was feeling matey and always used it when he wasn't.

'Not a cop. But I know some.'

'Where is she now, mate? Back at the flat?'

Flint glanced along the bar. Three of his mob had come in and were standing in a group at the far end, affecting to ignore Flint since he seemed in private conversation. Flint said,

'Look, mate, we don't want no bother, do we?'

'We don't want no bother,' agreed Sugden.

Flint put a hand on his arm.

'And the boys don't want no bother either, mate. They've just popped in for a peaceful drink, see? So where is she? I gotter special reason to pick her up. She wants her social contract, as she calls it. She can have it if she wants it. I'm going to marry her,' he said a little sheepishly, a little defiantly.

Sugden turned his head and looked him full in the eyes and said,

'If she's still around, that is.'

'Meaning what, mate?'

'Meaning if she's still alive. You half-sharp or something? Meaning if she's still alive.'

He saw Ron Flint blink and pressed his advantage.

'Meaning if she stays where she is, in our safe house, comfy and well-guarded, and doesn't do something daft and walk out or get picked up by you, she'll still be alive.'

He nodded towards the group at the bar and added,

'Think your mob could cope with what happened last night?'

Ron Flint looked down into his empty glass and said angrily,

'Tell her I said to say she's to stay where she is, tell her I said to say that, mate.'

'Think she'll agree?'

'If I said so, yes.'

'I don't,' Sugden said, and got up jingling his car keys and went out without there being any bother. He drove straight back to the office for his rendezvous with Vandoran, and for what lay ahead at the Raleigh Hotel at nine-thirty that night.

CHAPTER 14

The composition and texture of fear varies, ranging from the totally personal to an unselfish fear for somebody else's well-being.

There was a lot of it about now.

At heart Sugden did not care two pins about Edward 'Marsh' Mallow, M.P., or whether he lived or died. His respect for Vandoran was such that if Vandoran thought Mallow was a bad egg then that was good enough for Sugden, despite his protests.

Mallow could die and Sugden would lose no sleep. Sugden's fear was for Vandoran and the department. Vandoran's expressed intention to kill the man weighed on him like a dark, humid thunder-cloud, so that all the morning after he had fixed the appointment and during the afternoon and early evening he was conscious of feelings of oppression and depression.

Vandoran's refusal to discuss details was ominous. The killing of an M.P. was totally outrageous and was bound to backfire, leading not only to the ruin of Vandoran's career but future tiresome restrictions on the department's healthy extra-mural activities. He wouldn't get away with it. He couldn't get away with it.

Sugden saw no happy end to the story.

Fear was also swirling round the head of Edward Mallow when he replaced the telephone receiver after speaking to Sugden. Aged about thirty-eight, he had a slim, elegant figure and a curiously faun-like, sensitive-looking face, with a thin, straight nose and full pink lips and brown eyes which seemed to exude a gentle air of compassion and understanding on the world around him in general and on the person he was speaking to in particular. He had light-brown hair of a very fine, silky texture. As is often the nature of such fluffy hair, it was receding on either side of his forehead and thinning on the top of his head.

The Government was introducing a Bill for the compulsory control of the capsid moth among fruit growers' orchards, and although his Clapham, London, constituency could hardly be described as agricultural he was putting the finishing touches to a fairly powerful speech about the proliferation of regulations and the freedom of the individual when the telephone had interrupted him.

Now he pushed his notes aside and sat back, frowning, and running his slender fingers through the silky hair above his ears.

He knew his instructions, which were to ring his new controller in the event of being telephoned by anybody unknown to him personally. The names Sugden and Vandoran were certainly unknown to him.

Yet for some reason he was reluctant to do so.

He did not know the new man well. He called himself 'Peter', but he wasn't English. Unlike the warm, florid extrovert Ernest Markham the new man was phlegmatic, taciturn and, he felt, basically uninterested in his agent's personal life and fears.

Why did Ernest Markham have to go? It had worked so well, so smoothly, with Markham as controller and generous paymaster and Rachael Adams as courier, collecting the material and bringing the money if Markham was away. And why poor Richardson? A nice, loyal fellow. Completely discreet, utterly trustworthy. Why Richardson? And both so horribly, the one stabbed, the other bludgeoned. In each case it was supposed, no doubt, to be the action of a man in a rage, Father Brown being known to be quick-tempered. But so horrible, so very horrible.

Suddenly a thought occurred to him which made him feel momentarily a little sick. Rachael Adams and Ernest Markham both had duplicate keys to his flat, 'for your protection in case of emergency', Markham had said. It was always 'for your protection' when unusual requests were made.

The assassins could have entered quietly, unannounced. Had there been a ghastly mistake? Had Richardson been sitting with his back to them as they silently entered? Was he well known to the assassins? Had they known they were killing Richardson, or—? Or had they meant to kill him, Mallow? And if so, why? In heaven's name, why?

A few seconds' reflection reassured him. The value of the information he had given them over the previous four years was enormous. He knew that. It must have been, or they would not have paid him so much money. And you feed a goose with golden grain to make it lay golden eggs, you don't kill it.

The grain had been golden all right. He admitted that.

Not at first, of course. In the beginning it had been good, honest, undisguised blackmail, based on the fact that even in the present permissive age there were practices which were not likely to win votes in a general election even if now legal in private between consenting adult males.

But afterwards the corn had been tasty and he had enjoyed every golden grain of it. Moreover, each time, of recent years, when he had opened his beak and asked for more he had been given it – until the last occasion, a couple of days previously, when he had given rising inflation as an excuse for his demand.

He had been told by his new controller, a little curtly he thought, that the inflation was due to the capitalist system and it was his duty to help to destroy the system. There was no mention of more money.

Edward Mallow sighed. He didn't like the fellow but he would have to ring him. He picked up the telephone receiver and dialled Peter's number, and heard his wooden, unfriendly voice.

'Peter speaking. Yes?'

'I have had a call. Five minutes ago.'

'I know.'

'Then I do not need to repeat what was said.'

'Please repeat it. The monitoring was indistinct. Name of caller?'

'Sugden.'

There was silence for some seconds, then Peter said slowly,

'Please repeat the name and spell it.'

'Sugden. S-U-G-D-E-N.'

'Object of call?'

'He wishes to see me urgently. With a colleague.'

'Colleague in what?'

'He did not say.'

'Name?'

'Vandoran.'

'Please repeat and spell.'

'Vandoran. V-A-N-D-O-R-A-N.'

'You agreed to meet them?'

Mallow hesitated, licked his lips, and said,

'One thought it wise.'

'Correct. Meeting place? Date and time?'

'Here. My suite. This evening. Nine-thirty p.m. – twenty-one-thirty hours.'

'That is short notice.'

Edward Mallow heard a sound which he interpreted as

indicating annoyance. There was a long pause. One day he would have to have a showdown with the fellow, show him the facts of life, give him a bee and a flower, explain just who was doing a favour to whom. Now he said sharply,

'I tried to delay the meeting. I said I was going to Durham tomorrow and—'

'Are you?'

'Yes, I am. As you well know. He said it was urgent, they must come tonight.'

There was another long pause. He could imagine the man sitting at a desk, frowning, pulling at one of his long cigarettes.

'It is very inconvenient to me. It is very short notice.'

'It is very inconvenient to me, too,' Mallow said tartly, and added, 'they want to discuss—'

To his surprise he heard a short laugh.

'My friend, I *know* what they want to discuss, I know *that* all right, we heard *that* before somebody's damn radio interfered. That we know, that we know very well.'

'I take it I shall have the usual protection? Just in case?' When there was no immediate reply he repeated, in a louder tone, 'I take it I shall have the usual protection?'

To his surprise the reply now came quickly and in a soothing and friendly tone.

'It is not necessary, my friend – but yes, if you wish it, you shall have it. Goodbye.'

He heard a click, and replaced the handpiece of his own telephone and sat back, and felt a certain satisfaction. He had won a psychological battle with the man. Firmness had paid. He made a mental note of the fact for future occasions.

He went down in the lift and through the main hall on his way to the House of Commons. As he passed the reception-desk he saw the elegant figure and dark, swept-back hair of Rachael Adams behind the desk and smiled at her.

He had been instrumental at her request in getting her the job after the Markham tragedy and he was glad to see her. She was a link with the earlier, happier days when he had worked for old Ernest.

But he hadn't expected her to arrive so soon.

As his taxi bore him to Parliament Square worry swirled thinly round his brain. He hadn't expected to see her there until the next day. And mention of Father Brown was worrying.

Uneasily, he wondered if she was part of his protection or of his controller's – if she had been hurriedly sent to keep an eye open for British agents or to keep an eye on him.

His mind was not on the business of the House that day. He was too preoccupied with thinking about the evening meeting in his suite at the hotel.

And already a fall-back line of retreat was forming in his agile mind, in case something went wrong. The more he thought about it, the more he liked it. It might not even be a retreat. It might be a victory in the face of heavy odds.

The new Raleigh Hotel began life in 1962 in a hole in the ground to the north of Bayswater Road, in Cole Street, not far from Marble Arch. The hole in the ground bore some resemblance to the cavity left by an extracted tooth because a few weeks before the new Raleigh Hotel began to take shape there had been a solid though rather rambling old-fashioned predecessor, also called the Raleigh Hotel, of late-Victorian or early-Edwardian vintage.

The old hotel had a certain nostalgic charm for some

people. In the lounges in winter there were open, smoke-less, coal fires, and all the year round there was indifferently-cooked, unexciting food, bedside tables with chamber-pots, and an elderly staff of rheumy-eyed porters and waitresses and maids.

But to about fifty-seven elderly permanent residents, mostly women, it must have been regarded as home, since they grumbled among themselves about everything. Now and again there was one less grumbler and the coffin was brought downstairs at dinner-time so as not to upset the survivors. In 1960 the grumbling had to cease.

Some people in remote City offices had a long and con-genial lunch, haggled over a few figures, and forty elderly ladies and a few gentlemen were thrown out of what they regarded as a secure home; most of the rest followed soon afterwards, in ones and twos, like victims in tumbrils going to the guillotine, and about as cheerful.

The old Raleigh Hotel was demolished and the new one rose in all its majestic glory of steel and concrete. A hand-ful of the old residents had been lodged in another hotel owned by the new company, retained, as it were, for stock, and now these were sent back to the new Raleigh to salt the ground, because an entirely empty hotel is uninviting. So, it seemed, were the old residents, not being the right image for a modern hotel; and, as the hotel got going, they too had to get going in the end.

The final clear-out was completed when the hotel again changed hands, in 1965, and was acquired by yet another company, calling itself the London-Helsinki Hotel Com-pany. According to company particulars, the company existed 'to extend existing trade between Great Britain, Finland, and other Scandinavian countries, particularly in the hotel and restaurant business'. The new Raleigh Hotel was its first venture.

Vandoran and Sugden arrived at 9.15 p.m. in an office

car, and were openly set down by the driver at the main entrance. Vandoran said,

'We are early. Let us walk up and down. Let us take fresh air, Reg. Let us see what is to be seen. Above all, let us be seen by anybody who may be about to see us.'

He smiled and repeated the phrase: 'Above all, let us be seen by anybody who may be about to see us. We have been heard – at least you have, on the phone. Of that we can be sure. So now let us be seen.'

As they walked up one side of the road and down the other the first seedling of what Vandoran had in mind took firmer root in Sugden's brain, and he felt a pleasant increase in the tempo of his heart-beats in anticipation of what was ahead, though he had no idea of the exact shape of what was to come; and he did not ask because he knew that Vandoran would give an evasive answer. Sugden had learned by experience that Vandoran, like God, moved in a mysterious way his wonders to perform, but there were times when he wished that both of them would come out into the open a little more.

As they passed the hotel entrance a second time, Vandoran touched Sugden on the elbow and said, 'You will have observed the Swedish Volvo car we have just passed, and that it has two gentlemen seated in front?'

'I did – why?'

'Let us stop here while you relight your pipe.'

Sugden took out his lighter. He always kept the flame adjusted to the maximum height for his pipe and now, heated by the warmth of his pocket, the flame shot up high, hissing like a flame-thrower, illuminating his face with the square jaw, the straight nose, and his attempt to grow trendy hair around his ears and at the back of his neck.

It also lighted up Vandoran's less regular features. Sugden saw that there was no frog grin. Only the brown marble eyes were glinting malevolently.

They continued their walk to the corner of the road and paused, and as they looked back to the hotel entrance they saw the big Volvo car pull away from the side of the road and head north. Another car, a large Renault, which had been momentarily double-parked nearby, slid smoothly into the vacant place.

'Changing the guard, but not at Buckingham Palace,' muttered Vandoran.

'"Alice is marrying one of the Guards",' quoted Sugden softly. 'I've got a cousin called Alice. It's the sort of daft thing she might go and do, an' all. She'd never make a soldier's wife. I'd break her bloody neck if she tried to marry one of this guard.'

They walked back to the hotel and as they trod on the entrance mat and the swing doors swung automatically open they knew exactly what they would find inside.

A polished reception-desk with guide books and theatre advertisements, and rubber plants nearby. The central heating too hot. In the bedrooms, strips of impregnated paper so that guests could try and clean their shoes, free face tissues, little packs containing one or two buttons, a needle and cotton, and booklet matches with the name of the hotel on the front. At breakfast no generous slabs of butter but small rectangles wrapped in foil, and tiny plastic pots of marmalade. As clinically clean as a morgue awaiting its next guest. And as heartless.

Sugden went up to the reception-desk. A tall, slim young woman, with thick, dark hair swept back and tied at the back of her neck with a blue ribbon, got up from her chair and looked at him inquiringly. Sugden said,

'Mr Mallow, please. My name is Sugden. He is expecting me.'

She nodded and picked up a house telephone and dialled an extension and said, 'Mr Mallow? There is a

Mr Sugden and another gentleman here to see you. Mr Sugden says you are expecting him.'

She listened for a moment, replaced the receiver and said,

'Mr Mallow asks you to go up, sir. Fifth floor. Suite number one. A page will show you the way.'

'I can find my own way.'

She shrugged. 'The lifts are at the far end of the hall, sir, on the right.'

Sugden nodded and made his way to the lifts past a lounge where guests were sitting at small tables having drinks before going to bed. Most of them were obviously middle-aged married couples, though here and there were a few youngsters, probably Finns. Clean, healthy-looking young men and girls, probably enjoying a toot round London and getting rid of any inhibitions which they might have acquired at home.

On a settee at the corner where the lounge adjoined the passage leading to the lifts sat two men, aged about forty, chunky and grey-faced, unsmiling, with roving, watchful, blue eyes. They were drinking Coca-Cola.

In the lift Sugden said,

'He's well guarded.'

'Sacred cows are well guarded against every eventuality. Got a gun?'

'Of course not. You said—'

Vandoran nodded. 'I have. Incidentally, I'm going to wade straight in.'

Sugden shook his head despairingly, no longer impressed by his earlier idea of what was in Vandoran's mind. For a moment he began to wonder whether pressure of work was taking its toll of Vandoran's sanity. Usually they were on Christian-name terms but now, as if to impress on his superior the seriousness of his advice, he reverted to formality again.

'Look, sir, you can't kill an M.P.'

'You've said something of the sort once before.'

'You can't shoot an M.P. and get away with it,' said Sugden earnestly.

Normally Kenneth Vandoran had a clipped, almost metallic tone of voice; one of his colleagues said it reminded him of the bolt of a firearm being worked backwards and forwards. But now he spoke softly.

'There is no hundred per cent security in intelligence work. Now and again you *must* risk something – your job, your life, your—'

'Your sanity?' said Sugden, equally softly.

'I'm quite sane.'

'You could've kidded me,' Sugden murmured with a sinking heart.

Mr Edward 'Marsh' Mallow had rented a suite of two rooms and bathroom, as befitted a hard-working M.P. One room was his bedroom and the other his living and work-room. There was a communication door, and both rooms had a door opening on to a small hall and thence to the corridor.

He met his visitors at the lift and with a perfunctory word of greeting led them into the living-room, furnished with the usual modern hotel type of table, chairs, desk and television set. Most of the furniture looked as though it were made of hardboard with a polished veneer of unknown composition.

Sugden had not tried very hard to imagine what a sacred cow looked like. If he had had to define such thoughts as he had on the subject he would have been inclined to describe not so much a sacred cow as a modified version of a Cretan bull, complete with labyrinth and with a built-in readiness to approve any normal quota of victims deemed necessary for his well-being. In human terms he thought of a tough, squat man of about forty-five, with cunning, suspicious eyes, a blue jowl and a generally ruthless air. Therefore he was surprised at Mallow's appearance, at his faun-like, sensitive-looking face, full lips and soft brown eyes.

Mallow flung himself down into the chair before the writing-desk, ran his slender fingers through his light-brown, silky hair, and deprecated the place in which he was receiving his visitors.

'One is conscious of the barbarian nature of so many modern hotels,' he said sadly.

His voice was low and modulated, so that Sugden had the impression that he was not so much blaming the creators of the hotels as the fabric of present-day life which appeared to welcome such places.

Mallow sighed. 'But one had to go somewhere, hadn't one? One couldn't, one really couldn't go back to that flat, after that ghastly tragedy – not until it had been thoroughly cleaned up and redecorated, but absolutely entirely redecorated. So here one is for one's sins, isn't one?'

Vandoran smiled. The smile was deceptive.

'What sins?'

'I beg your pardon?'

Vandoran turned his head slightly towards Sugden.

'Doors,' he said.

Sugden got up from his chair.

'The doors are shut,' Mallow said. Sugden took no notice, going to both doors and pushing the bolts forward. He sat down saying, 'That's it, then. Nobody can disturb us.'

Mallow sat upright in his chair, features immobile. He said, 'I didn't ask you to bolt them. One doesn't like locked doors.'

'Aye, well, they're bolted now, whether one does or one doesn't.'

'What sins?' asked Vandoran again.

'A figure of speech one often uses. Doesn't one?'

Vandoran said nothing. He unbuttoned his jacket, groped with his right hand, and took the Mauser automatic from the shoulder-holster and laid it on his lap, still saying nothing.

Mallow stared at it. Then he leaned forward in his chair, his face rigid, his brown eyes were no longer soft, compassionate, or understanding, but calculating and as hard as Vandoran's. Nor was that the only resemblance between them. When he spoke his voice was now as metallic as Vandoran's.

'If this is a prelude to a hold-up you can save your time. There is nothing here worth taking.'

'Except your life.'

'And that's not worth much, but it's better than nowt,' added Sugden.

Mallow said, 'I think you had better go,' and he leaned over towards his desk and reached for the telephone, ignoring Vandoran, ignoring the Mauser, ignoring Sugden, too, not knowing that a bulky figure can leap like a kangaroo if really pressed, only knowing that his right hand and wrist, extended towards the 'phone, were held fast, then twisted, and the twist extended now from the wrist to the forearm, and unless he could bear the pain and the prospect of even more pain till the arm was dislocated he must turn his body and sink to the floor by the desk. Sugden pushed the 'phone to the back of the desk.

'Don't try that again, that's daft, that is.'

'Get up,' Vandoran said and waved his automatic, first at Mallow and then at the desk chair. 'Get up and sit down.'

'You don't look dignified down there,' Sugden said. 'Not like an M.P. should look, you don't, sprawling over the floor. Get up like Mr Vandoran says, and no funny business.'

Sugden saw a slight movement of the thumb of Vandoran's right hand and thought, Oh my God, he's pushed the safety-catch on the Mauser. He's going to do it now, he's going to shoot him sitting in his chair, full-face.

Why had Vandoran been so cagey, why had he said, 'Leave the details to me,' when it was all going to be so straightforward? Sugden averted his head slightly, not so far that he couldn't see Mallow out of the corners of his eyes, just in case of trouble, but sufficiently to avoid seeing the terror in the man's eyes and the hole in the broad forehead which must appear.

He held his breath and clenched his teeth so that the muscles at the sides of his face ached. Sugden had no fear when it came to an active gun fight. But he had no stomach for a cold-blooded execution. There would be noise, of course, noise from the shot – or shots, if another were necessary to finish him off – and perhaps noise from Mallow, come to that, but nobody in the hotel would bat an eyelid thanks to all the violence and noise on television.

Sugden heard Mallow say, 'No, don't,' and guessed he also had seen Vandoran shift the safety-catch. Then he heard him say 'No, please don't,' and wished Vandoran would get on with it, get it over and done with. And suddenly, in the instant of waiting, Sugden realised that although he himself would not do the shooting it was he, Sugden, who had given his real name to the girl at the desk and it was he, Sugden, who would have to do the talking later, to the girl and to the police, and for the first time he almost wished he had never met Vandoran.

But he heard no shot. Instead of a shot and a scream he heard Vandoran's voice,

'Where's the priest? Where's Lawrence Brown?' And he caught Mallow's shaky reply, 'I don't know. I promise I don't know, if I knew I would tell you. What was done to him was partly to protect me, in the past one has—'

'Yes,' said Vandoran in his metallic voice. 'One knows.'

'One knows all that, one does,' Sugden said. 'Does one know any other reason?'

Mallow glanced from one to the other, knowing Sugden was mocking his affected speech but also knowing he had gained a respite. He said,

'It is only a guess – from something Ernest Markham said. Poor Ernest.'

'What did poor Ernest say?' Vandoran asked. 'Tell us what poor Ernest said.' He laid the Mauser on his lap again. Mallow noted the movement and tried to regain some dignity.

'Who are you? Police?'

'Not police,' said Vandoran.

'Worse,' said Sugden and gave a short hard laugh. 'Worse than police – from your point of view. What did poor Ernest say?'

Mallow shook his head. 'Nothing.'

'You said he did,' Vandoran said. 'We don't seem to be getting anywhere, do we?' He spoke mildly, letting his right hand drop down to the Mauser on his lap. Mallow said hastily,

'One day I said, "Is a lot done to protect me?" and he said, "Mostly to protect you." He emphasised the *you*, and I said, "What other reason?"'

'What did he reply?'

'He said, "Mind your own business." Like that. Sharpish.'

Vandoran looked at Sugden. He said,

'I think he's lying. Mr Mallow is lying.'

'No doubt about it,' Sugden said. 'Daft, really.'

Vandoran nodded and said, 'They get away with so much.'

'Get over-confident, that's their trouble,' Sugden said, 'Not that it makes any difference now.'

'None at all. He's got to go.'

'This evening,' agreed Vandoran.

'Why not now? What are we waiting for?' asked Sugden briskly, hoping that Vandoran was bluffing.

'If you don't want to watch,' said Vandoran delicately, 'you can go and use his portable typewriter over there. The usual suicide note. Distressed at the death of his dear friend. Life no longer worth living. All that stuff. Balance of mind disturbed. Gun by his side.' He glanced down at the Mauser on his lap. 'Pity to lose it. It's an old friend. But I'll have to leave it with the body.'

Edward Mallow had been listening, glancing from one to the other, eyes hard and alert, thin nose raised, testing the wind, trying to gauge the degree of danger. It was the mention of the suicide note which decided him.

He leaned forward in his chair. Now was the moment for the fall-back plan which wasn't a plan for retreat, which he had decided upon in the taxi to the House of Commons, which could turn defeat and peril into victory.

'I guessed it would come to this in the end,' Mallow said and Sugden, who was about to get up and move to the portable typewriter to tap out the suicide note, leaned back in his chair once more and looked at Mallow.

'Come to what, then?'

'This. I'm glad you're here, you know.'

Sugden laughed. 'You've got funny tastes, you have.'

Vandoran looked at Mallow with his almond eyes expressionless.

'Explain, please.'

'One has been thinking about it for some time.'

'One has?' sneered Sugden. 'No doubt one has made out one's Will? And lodged it in one's bank?' He was at sea now, knowing only that he must play along with Vandoran. He saw Mallow take a deep breath, heard him say,

'It has been on my conscience. Now I will make amends, now I will make restitution.'

'Go on,' Vandoran said coldly. 'Make your approach, do your fan dance.'

'Fan dance?'

'What sort of muck are you going to offer? What kind of chicken-feed are you going to toss me in return for your life?'

He patted the Mauser on his lap. 'I shall be sorry to leave this behind. It has killed bigger rats in its time.'

Edward Mallow searched Vandoran's face. He saw neither interest nor pity. He felt worried and afraid, yet at the same time he was alert, conscious of the ammunition still at his disposal. Indeed, in a way the presence of the danger and fear afforded him an odd, almost masochistic, excitement. There were, he knew, people who had drawn similar excitement from the terrors of war-time bombing raids. He had not understood this before. Now, fleetingly, he did.

'I will not offer you chicken-feed,' he said loudly. 'I will offer you, here, now, some good *hors d'œuvre.*'

Vandoran looked at his watch. 'You have two minutes.'

Mallow said quickly,

'The company which owns this hotel is based in Helsinki, and Finland is close to Russia.'

'Thank you for telling me that.'

'Ernest Markham and I hold a majority of shares in this hotel. I should say – I *do*. And poor Ernest *did*. We did between us.'

'Thank you for telling me what I knew already from

company particulars furnished to the authorities. You are not doing well.'

Edward Mallow licked his lips. It didn't matter, it didn't matter at all, the best was still to come.

'The hotel is to be used as a safe place in which to brief and de-brief their agents, and accommodate visiting intelligence officers.'

Vandoran affected to yawn.

'Even a child could assume that. And don't tell me Markham gave you the money to acquire the shares because a child could assume that, too. And I am no teenager. And don't tell me half the hotel employees are K.G.B. agents installed through your influence, because our time is precious. Yours is, anyway.'

He looked at his watch again.

'What happened to the priest?'

Mallow shook his head. 'I have told you – I don't know.'

'Pity. It's the one thing I wanted to know.'

Mallow said urgently, 'The Catholic and General Publishing Company attracted many interesting people who might later be approached for other things. Everyone thinks he can write a book, Mr Vandoran.'

Vandoran said nothing. He did not seem remotely interested. But at length he said in a bored voice, 'Now you are going to tell me something else which I guessed, aren't you? You are going to give me the remarkable information that it was obvious that Father Brown would write a book because he would need money. Therefore it was better that it should be edited and published under Markham's control. So Markham wrote to Father Brown under K.G.B. instructions.'

Vandoran paused and added, 'Is that all that you would have included among the *hors d'œuvre*?'

He didn't wait for an answer. He said,

'The *hors d'œuvre* are not good, Mr Mallow.'

'Fishy,' said Sugden, backing him up. 'Too much fish. Give you belly-wauch, they do.'

'Not fishy,' Vandoran said. 'Tasteless.'

'Old dead-beat stuff,' Sugden said.

'Stale,' Vandoran said. 'Known already.'

'Worthless,' Sugden said.

Mallow looked from one to the other. Now was the moment. The bombers were overhead. He felt the perverse excitement of intense, throbbing danger, heard his heart-beats pounding in his ears, knew that there comes a moment when you either dived for the bomb shelter or decided to come down with the building.

He had no intention of coming down with the building. He intended to emerge triumphant when the raid was over. He said quickly,

'I can help you in a big way, Mr Vandoran.'

'Not from where I'm viewing the scene.'

'I am prepared to join your staff, Mr Vandoran.'

He sat back to watch the effect of his words.

Vandoran laid the Mauser automatic on the carpet by his chair. He had no immediate use for it. Mallow's eyes gleamed softly, moistly. Now he could come out of his bomb shelter, and press his advantage as he had planned to do, if necessary.

'There are, of course, conditions. Mr Markham was generous with money – and shares. No doubt you will be, too. I shall naturally require a regular consultancy fee, perhaps seven thousand pounds a year, rising with inflation.'

Vandoran raised his glance from the floor where the Mauser lay.

'I don't invest in dead ducks,' he said.

Mallow looked at the Mauser automatic lying on the carpet, then at Vandoran, then at Sugden who held no fire-arm, then back at Vandoran. He seemed genuinely surprised.

'Dead ducks?'

'You're a dead duck.'

'And not even edible,' Sugden said.

Vandoran glanced vaguely round the room.

'How many microphones do you reckon there are in this joint, Reg?'

Sugden thought for a moment, looking round as Vandoran had done.

'Maybe four, maybe five. Two in this room, one in the bedroom, one in the hall, perhaps one in the bathroom.'

Mallow laughed. A cunning look came into his eyes. He said softly,

'Certainly the place is bugged – for my own protection. But I switch off when I wish. Come, I will show you, the switch is in the bathroom cupboard.'

He made to rise from his chair. Vandoran waved him back.

'Don't bother. It's a toy. To make you happy. You can flick it up and down as much as you like, if it makes you happy. It makes no bloody difference.'

He saw the uncertainty begin to creep back into Mallow's face.

'They wouldn't dare,' Mallow murmured. 'They trust me, they need me, I'm important, they wouldn't dare!'

'They wouldn't dare *not* to. You're an important agent. You said so,' Vandoran said.

'You were,' said Sugden. 'You *were* important.'

'I don't take on people with no life expectancy,' Vandoran said, and picked up the automatic from the floor and saw the fear flooding back into Mallow's face. 'Don't worry, I'm not going to kill you. I'll leave it to the others. They've had more practice.'

He gazed at Mallow thoughtfully.

'I wouldn't give much for you at an auction.'

'Collector's piece?' suggested Sugden. 'Rarity value?'

Mallow said loudly, shrilly, 'I don't believe this place is bugged – unless it's by you!'

'There's one born every minute,' Sugden said.

'We don't bug M.P.s' flats,' Vandoran said primly. 'You should know that.'

'Some mothers have 'em, this bloke's mother had a beaut,' Sugden said rudely.

Extract from official report prepared for the Home Secretary by Kenneth Vandoran:

Subject subsequently became seriously disturbed by the course which events had taken and the possible consequences. He repeated that he could be of assistance to me, but I again declined his offer. Subject then became tearful and hysterical, and begged me to arrest him for his own safety. I replied that in view of his position as a member of Her Majesty's Opposition I felt that I should have authorisation to request the police to make the arrest, such being the correct procedure. He retorted that every citizen had powers of arrest, but I pointed out to him that such powers depended upon a citizen discovering another person in the act of committing a criminal act and that he, Mr Mallow, was not at that moment committing such an act. I would, however, take appropriate action upon leaving the hotel.

Subject then became confused about his immediate plans. He went into the bedroom and began to toss certain articles of apparel and personal belongings into a suitcase but abandoned this operation after a few minutes, stating that he must leave the hotel at once.

He returned to the sitting-room and seemed about to

exhort me further when the telephone-bell rang. It appeared from the one-sided conversation available to me that it was the reception desk informing him that some person or persons wished to see him. I heard what sounded like the name Peter spoken by the receptionist.

Mr Mallow replied that his present visitors would be leaving in about five minutes and he would ring down when he was free. This he clearly had no intention of doing since he went into the bedroom and collected his suitcase and such things as were in it. He was again in a tearful and hysterical condition which in certain circumstances would have been distressing to observe.

He announced his intention of leaving the suite when we did. I expressed doubt as to whether he would be able to leave the hotel unmolested, considering who was running it, but he made mention of a fire exit along the landing.

Mr Sugden and I, accompanied by Mr Mallow, then went into the hall. At this point subject said that in his haste he had forgotten his briefcase containing a considerable quantity of money and some interesting documents. He turned back towards his bedroom.

I opened the front door and was surprised to find a young lady, whom I recognised as the receptionist, and two gentlemen unknown to me standing on the threshold. They stood aside to allow us to come on to the landing. The lady said Mr Mallow was expecting them. I said I believed he was.

I ventured to add, '*Détente!* Anglo-Russian co-operation. He is all yours.'

Later, while waiting for the lift, we heard what appeared to be a shot from a pistol or revolver.

CHAPTER 15

Vandoran was sitting at his desk glancing through the morning papers while his senior frogs filed in for the daily conference known irreverently to the staff as the early-morning prayer meeting. When they were seated round his desk he pushed the last of the newspapers aside and gave one of his wide, amphibian smiles.

'Owing to Mr Mallow's suicide – for that lad certainly brought about his own death – there will now be a by-election down Clapham way.'

He paused and looked Sugden full in the face.

'I said I'd kill him. There's more than one way of killing a sacred cow.' He paused, no longer smiling. 'I am sorry about Ernest Markham.'

'I'm not, I'm not bloody sorry at all,' Sugden said.

Vandoran turned a disapproving face towards him.

'You should be,' he said. 'Jews. He and Rachael Adams, both Jews. With relatives – over there.'

He picked up a framed photograph of a labour camp which, with other photos, always stood on his desk.

'How would you react, Reg? What would you answer if one day one of that lot came to you and said, "Either you help us or some of your relations—"' He stopped.

Sugden shook his head. He knew Vandoran's temperament, the curious mixture of ruthlessness and unexpected humanity, and he wasn't being drawn into a fight.

Sugden said, 'Aye, well, I'll deal with that sort of thing if it comes. I shoot the nearest shark's fin, like you said. Anyway, we've killed the sacred cow, so that's that.'

'It isn't a case of *that's that* at all,' Vandoran said sharply, and gazed round at his silent frogs.

'Mallow was an important agent. So important that two men are killed to protect him; and in the process a priest is framed and then kidnapped, and an attempt is made to do away with the priest's floozie. Suddenly Peter, the new controller, grows cool towards Mallow – for whose security so much had been done. Then he is killed. What does that suggest?'

An up-and-coming frog with eyes on promotion cleared his throat. Vandoran looked towards him.

'Well?'

'It suggests to me, sir, that Mallow was no longer necessary, that *there is another sacred cow, perhaps bigger*; that rightly or wrongly they thought it possible that Mallow might or might not have an inkling of who it is. They were taking no chances.'

Vandoran nodded approvingly.

'I concur. So it's not a matter of *that's that*. It's a question of what's next? And *where? And who?*'

'And talking of where, where's the priest?' muttered Sugden.

Vandoran picked a typed sheet from his in-tray and held it in his left hand; in his right hand he held the Nazi dagger and beat a faint tattoo with the point on the polished desk.

'This is a transcript of last night's monitored broadcast from over there. "Father Lawrence Brown, a former Roman Catholic priest in London, made the following statement tonight. For reasons unknown to me, but doubtless because I had left the Catholic church for a woman I dearly loved, I was framed recently in London, and the police sought me in connection with two murders I had not committed.

'"Having no faith in the capitalist system of justice

and, owing to prejudice, expecting none in the position in which I found myself, I accepted outside assistance and finally agreed to leave England discreetly and take up a position here of religious adviser, specialising in the Catholic Church, both Roman and Greek Orthodox, and its imperialist machinations and capitalist intrigues. I am convinced that this can be my humble contribution to peace. I regret my past political mistakes and welcome this great chance to make amends." '

There was dead silence. Vandoran said, 'They didn't do a bad job – for us, anyway. And apart from anything else, there's some propaganda value for *them* in robbing an R.C. priest. Odd story, sad in a way.' Sugden stirred slightly and said,

'He always wanted to be a somebody.' He looked at Vandoran and said in his usual, tactless Yorkshire way, 'You said he was dead. I doubted it. You were wrong, I was right.'

Vandoran gave one of his more malevolent smiles.

'I hope he lives a long time,' he said. 'And I hope he is happy,' he added insincerely. 'Over there, they have a name for people like him. They call them, "the living dead", because they can never, ever leave the country. You were right – but I was not wrong.'

No frog dared to laugh.

F   M   8257
B

Bingham, John

Ministry of Death

DATE DUE

FEB 1 7 1978	JAN 2		
MAR 1 8 1978	SEP 5 '80 JAN 20 '81		
APR 1 1978	FEB 14 '89		
APR 2 4 1978	JUN 2 2 1984		
MAY 8 1978	Jul 10 84		
MAY 2 3 1978	JAN 3 1989		
JUN 6 1978			
JUN 3 0 1978			